Jessie was thrown from her seat
by the sudden application
of the train brakes.

The squeal of the brakes was quickly joined by the screams of frightened passengers. There was a brief moment of calm as the train skidded to a stop, but it was shattered by a sudden crash. Ki immediately went to Jessie's aid, but she was already pulling herself up into her seat.

"They may be hurt up front," he said hastily. He raced from the car, and as he dropped down to the roadbed, a powerful explosion nearly knocked him off his feet. The bursting steam boiler sealed the fate of the hapless engineer and fireman, but he continued to rush ahead.

Ki walked around the front of the engine and froze in his tracks. *This horrible incident was not an accident,* Ki thought. *This was cold-blooded murder!*

Also in the LONE STAR series
from Jove

LONGARM AND THE LONE STAR LEGEND
LONE STAR ON THE TREACHERY TRAIL
LONE STAR AND THE RENEGADE COMANCHES
LONE STAR ON OUTLAW MOUNTAIN
LONGARM AND THE LONE STAR VENGEANCE
LONE STAR AND THE GOLD RAIDERS
LONE STAR AND THE DENVER MADAM
LONE STAR AND THE RAILROAD WAR
LONE STAR AND THE MEXICAN STANDOFF
LONE STAR AND THE BADLANDS WAR
LONE STAR AND THE SAN ANTONIO RAID
LONE STAR AND THE GHOST PIRATES
LONE STAR ON THE OWLHOOT TRAIL
LONGARM AND THE LONE STAR BOUNTY
LONE STAR ON THE DEVIL'S TRAIL
LONE STAR AND THE APACHE REVENGE
LONE STAR AND THE TEXAS GAMBLER
LONE STAR AND THE HANGROPE HERITAGE
LONE STAR AND THE MONTANA TROUBLES
LONE STAR AND THE MOUNTAIN MAN
LONE STAR AND THE STOCKYARD SHOWDOWN
LONE STAR AND THE RIVERBOAT GAMBLERS
LONE STAR AND THE MESCALERO OUTLAWS
LONE STAR AND THE AMARILLO RIFLES
LONE STAR AND THE SCHOOL FOR OUTLAWS
LONE STAR ON THE TREASURE RIVER
LONE STAR AND THE MOON TRAIL FEUD
LONE STAR AND THE GOLDEN MESA
LONGARM AND THE LONE STAR RESCUE
LONE STAR AND THE RIO GRANDE BANDITS
LONE STAR AND THE BUFFALO HUNTERS
LONE STAR AND THE BIGGEST GUN IN THE WEST
LONE STAR AND THE APACHE WARRIOR
LONE STAR AND THE GOLD MINE WAR
LONE STAR AND THE CALIFORNIA OIL WAR
LONE STAR AND THE ALASKAN GUNS
LONE STAR AND THE WHITE RIVER CURSE
LONGARM AND THE LONE STAR DELIVERANCE
LONE STAR AND THE TOMBSTONE GAMBLE
LONE STAR AND THE TIMBERLAND TERROR
LONE STAR IN THE CHEROKEE STRIP

WESLEY ELLIS

LONE STAR

AND THE OREGON RAIL SABOTAGE

A JOVE BOOK

LONE STAR AND THE OREGON RAIL SABOTAGE

A Jove Book / published by arrangement with
the author

PRINTING HISTORY
Jove edition / May 1986

ISBN: 0-515-08570-7

Jove Books are published by The Berkley Publishing Group,
200 Madison Avenue, New York, N.Y. 10016.

PRINTED IN THE UNITED STATES OF AMERICA

For my father,
who told me his stories
of the trail.

And for Carol,
who listened to mine.

LONE STAR
AND THE OREGON RAIL SABOTAGE

Chapter 1

The black, sooty smoke drifted to the heavens as the locomotive thundered through the mountain pass. Dotting the slope on either side of the tracks, magnificent evergreens towered up to the clear, blue skies. On the surrounding mountains, the spring run-off was lacing the snow-capped peaks with dozens of cascading, iridescent waterfalls.

Looking out the window of the Pullman, Jessica Starbuck marveled at the vast panorama that sped past. Keeping her eyes toward the window, she addressed the tall, muscular gentleman sitting next to her.

"Quite a change from the Circle Star isn't it, Ki?"

Ki, the half Japanese, half American full-time companion and bodyguard to Jessie, nodded his head. "Very majestic."

And as the mountains were impressively majestic, so Jessie was noteworthily statuesque. Her green tweed jacket and matching skirt cloaked her rounded firm figure, and her tawny blond hair fell freely to her shoulders. It was her most striking feature—until one caught sight of her sparkling, bright green eyes. She turned her eyes from the view. "But I still like the Circle Star."

"There's no place like home." Ki's voice had a hint of that plaintive tone that only the truly homeless can seem to manage. Although the Texas ranch was like a home to him, it was still an adopted one. Years earlier, Ki, an outcast in his own country, had been taken in by Alex Starbuck, Jessie's father. He was hired as a bodyguard, but he had become a friend.

Jessie smiled. "You just echoed what Alex often said." Her voice trailed off and she turned to stare out the window. Ki accepted the compliment silently, careful not to intrude on Jessie's thoughts. Eventually the *clickety-clack* of the rails brought Jessie from the thoughts of her murdered father back to the here and now. As Ki had taught her, the past, the present and the future are forever entwined. At this moment they were riding the Oregon Short Line to go to the aid of an old family friend.

"Did you ever meet Commodore Whiting?" Jessie asked Ki.

"No, but your father spoke of him often," Ki replied.

"He believed the railroads would open the gates to the West. They laid a lot of tracks together, those two."

"And now you're continuing," added Ki.

"We're supplying financial support—"

Ki raised an eyebrow. "If walking into the middle of a rail war is just financial support—"

"Why, Ki, I thought after that last dusty cattle drive you'd find the cool northern air a refreshing change."

They were both grinning. Ki added a final cryptic note to their exchange. "You always have a way of smelling out the skunk."

Jessie smiled—snarled, actually. The construction of the Wood River Railway, a branch line of the Oregon Short Line was being financed by Starbuck Enterprises. Its completion would enable them to ship their lumber economically from their mills to the cities of the East. But laying the tracks had been going slowly. Sabotage was the presumed cause, and although rail wars were common, Jessie suspected it was more than that. The timbered landscape that glided past focused Jessie's attention on the need to protect the Starbuck lumber venture. Jessie possessed a sixth sense, and she intuited that this was not a rail war, but part of the continuing battle between Starbuck Enterprises and the Prussian-based cartel that first murdered her mother and then her father and hoped ultimately to gain financial and political control of the United States. When Jessie inherited the Starbuck empire, she inherited the unspoken legacy always to thwart the lawless international syndicate. And Jessie was not one to back down from a fight, especially with the cartel.

She turned back to Ki, but just as she was about to speak, she was thrown from her seat by the sudden application of the train brakes. The squeal of the brakes was quickly joined by the screams of frightened passengers. There was a brief moment of calm as the train skidded to a stop, but it was shattered by a sudden crash. While the impact sent most everybody hurling to the floor, Ki was nimbly getting to his feet. Rather than resisting the jolt, Ki went with the force. By lowering his center of gravity and shifting his balance, a smooth rolling somersault was all that was needed to put him on his feet. He immediately went to Jessie's aid, but she was already pulling herself up into her seat.

"They may be hurt up front," Ki said hastily. No further explanation was needed or given. Ignoring the shocked passengers, Ki raced from the car; Jessie would take care of them. As he dropped down to the roadbed, a powerful explosion nearly knocked him off his feet. Up ahead, jets of steam sprayed the air. The bursting steam boiler practically sealed the fate of the hapless engineer and fireman, but Ki continued to rush ahead. There was always a slim chance someone was thrown far enough to survive the explosion.

When he reached the wreckage, it was all too easy to piece together the gruesome details. The engineer was standing at the controls, his hands locked around the brake stick. His diligent fight right up to the last was the only thing that had saved the train from total destruction. It pained Ki to see such a brave soul crushed dead between the fire wall and tender. And it took only a moment for Ki to spot the lifeless form of the fireman twenty yards away. He was wrapped around the trunk of a tall pine, his neck probably broken.

Ki walked around the front of the engine and froze in his tracks. This horrible incident was not an accident. Lying across the tracks was a pile of timber. It constituted a virtually impassable barrier. With the logs placed very close to the last bend, there was never a chance to stop the train in time.

No, this was no accident, Ki thought. This was cold-blooded murder.

So intent was Ki in his investigation that he failed to hear the approach of three men on horseback. With guns drawn, they entered the back of the coach. Inside, the car was a scene of confusion. Injured passengers were lying about moaning. Scared children were crying and desperately seeking attention. A shrieking baby ignored his mother's efforts to comfort him. Luckily the car was nearly empty. Only a handful of businessmen and a few families ventured this far along the branch line.

Jessie knelt over an elderly woman and was wiping blood from the woman's cut brow with her handkerchief. Others were also attending to the needs of the injured.

There was such commotion that the holdup men went unnoticed at first. The leader of the bandits, a heavyset man chomping on a cigar, finally raised his gun and fired a shot. All heads turned.

"Everyone back in your seats, now!" His voice was thick and heavy.

The stunned passengers were slow to move. The gunman took two steps down the aisle, grabbed a young man, and threw him forcefully back into his seat. As he grabbed a woman and threw her, the other passengers started to move back to their seats.

"We're takin' up a collection for our Sunday prayer meetin' and we want all to be right generous." His filthy, tobacco-stained teeth showed briefly as his lips parted in a smile. He nodded to a companion to begin taking the passengers' money.

"Follow directions and no one'll get hurt," he barked, then turned to the third gunman, a tall lanky fellow, and issued further instructions. "Take care of the rear brakeman." The man left without delay.

The collection was going smoothly and speedily. The gunman would press his six-shooter into a man's face and hold it there until he had emptied the contents of his billfold or money purse into the gunman's overturned Stetson. Only when he was satisfied would the gunman move on to the next donor.

Meanwhile, Jessie waited patiently for her turn. She had a special surprise strapped to the inside of her thigh, a two-shot, ivory-handled derringer. At point-blank range she could dispose of the one bandit quickly and turn her last shot on the leader before he was wise to what had happened.

But before reaching Jessie, the bandit noticed a figure hunched behind a seat. Pointing his gun, he called loudly, "C'mon out, hands high."

From behind the seat a woman's voice answered, "This man's shoulder's broken; he can't be moved."

Slowly the woman stood up. She had dark curly hair tied back in a bow and equally dark, big brown eyes. She was short and well proportioned with a narrow waist and full, round breasts that pressed against her plain calico dress. More important, she was young and pretty and had an air of defiance that was sure to get her in trouble.

The bandit lowered his gun and approached her. "Maybe we got ourselves something extra this time, eh, boss?" he said and smiled wickedly.

"We ain't got time for that," the leader replied.

"Aw, c'mon, Smokey, you don't see a pretty thing like this at Fannie's."

"Shut up!" the leader barked.

The bandit was clumsily pawing at the woman's breasts. "It won't take long and we ain't had no fun since—"

"All right, we'll take her with us," the leader consented.

With a smile that was to be the last of his life, the bandit grabbed the dress, pulling at the neckline. There was a short rip and then a high-pitched whine. He let go of the dress and clutched at his throat. Imbedded deep into his jugular was a small, star-shaped blade, one of Ki's deadly *shuriken* throwing stars. He dropped to the floor, a smile frozen on his lifeless face.

Smokey did not hear Ki, nor the sound of the *shuriken*, but he did see his pal drop. But by then it was too late. Before the bandit had hit the floor, Jessie had her derringer out. There were two sharp cracks. The bandit leader fell over backward, his .45 exploding pointlessly into the roof. In the center of his forehead was a small, black hole. An inch higher, just under the hairline, was another hole.

The sound of a rapidly galloping horse shook Jessie out of her momentary calm. She grabbed one bandit's Colt and went rushing to a window. The third bandit was making a quick getaway. She took aim, sighting carefully, but Ki was at her side, placing a restraining hand over her arm.

"Let him go," he said softly. "If they're cartel men, let this be a warning."

Jessie smiled. "Our calling card may force them into the open."

Ki nodded. "Any serious injuries?" he asked.

"Not to any of the passengers," Jessie answered with a smirk. "The best thing for us is to head out to the railhead." She gestured to the two dead holdup men, "There should be two horses outside. We'll make it in a few hours, and they'll have a crew out here by evening."

They turned from the window and headed to the door.

Then Ki got a good look at the woman he had saved. Heedless of her torn dress and half-exposed breasts, she was approaching him.

"Thank you," she said somewhat shyly. Ki couldn't help but notice her heaving bosom. "My name's Cynthia." She leaned over and kissed him on the cheek. "I wish I could thank you proper," she whispered in his ear. Her soft breasts pressed against Ki's chest, and as she stepped back her erect nipples brushed lightly against him, leaving him slightly embarrassed and highly aroused. He nodded politely and then followed Jessie out the door.

Chapter 2

Jessie and Ki made good time. The sun was still high in the sky when they spied the construction camp in the distance. The sight of the dozen large tents came as no surprise, for Ki had heard the rhythmic *clang* of hammer hitting spike a few miles back; sound traveled far in the thin mountain air.

They had been moving fast, but now Jessie reined in her brown gelding. There was no sense working the horse into the ground, and the slower pace allowed Jessie to study the camp and its rush of activity. Off to the side of some tents stood a half dozen small shacks, probably used for equipment and supplies. There was also a very large lumberyard set behind the camp, and along the tracks was a row of open gondolas on sidings and filled with crushed rock.

But what caught her eye was the syncopated dancelike maneuvers of those laying track. From the distance they seemed like worker ants swarming over an ant hill. Six men, three on a side, would grab a steel rail, run it up to the end of the track, and drop it. There, other men working in pairs would place the spikes and drive them home. Meanwhile, a steady stream of men would rush forth with wooden ties and place them across the gravel roadbed. By the time the last spike was in place, another rail, brought up by six more railbearers, was already in position. And so it went, the railroad moving constantly forward.

Laying of the track was one part of the work. Mule-driven wagons were carting timber into the lumberyard, a hub of equal activity. There, the men were divided into groups who unloaded the raw timber, sawed the wood into ties and posts, and stacked the lumber for later use. Rounding out the business of building a railroad were another twenty men busy crushing rock with heavy mallets.

Jessie turned to Ki. "Looks like everything is running smoothly," she said.

"If everything were running smoothly, we wouldn't be here," replied Ki.

Jessie started to give Ki a sharp look. She didn't need to be reminded of the obvious, but she broke into a smile—once she saw Ki's raised eyebrows and innocent shrug of the shoulders. There was something almost laughable about such a childish gesture in such a powerful man.

From afar Jessie and Ki had drawn little attention. There was nothing odd about two persons on horseback. Before they set out, Jessie had changed into her riding clothes. She was now comfortably attired in tight, well-worn denim pants and a denim jacket. She wore riding boots of cordovan leather, and a polished holster of matching leather was strapped to her hip. In the holster rested her custom Colt .38, its burnished peachwood handle looking very much at home against her soft, rounded hip. As they approached, Jessie, no longer mistaken by some for a man, turned more than a few heads.

As they passed a loaded wagon, Jessie called out to the admiring teamster, "Gil Johnson?"

"Over that way, ma'am, in the caboose." He pointed to

a caboose set off on the siding. Jessie nodded her thanks and reined her horse in that direction. The teamster continued to stare after her and was nearly thrown from his wagon when it hit a hole.

As Jessie and Ki dismounted in front of the caboose, a tall, broad-shouldered man, his right arm in a sling, stepped out to greet them. He had dark, curly hair and a strong, straight forehead. He wasn't unduly handsome, but he had an air of competence to him that made him more attractive than his average good looks. Jessie tried to guess his age; his eyes, a warm brown, had a youthful look to them, but his face was lined by experience.

Smiling, he slipped his arm from the sling and extended his hand, "Miss Starbuck? I'm Gil Johnson." He saw her concern for his arm and explained quickly, "It was coming off tomorrow anyway."

After hearing his voice, Jessie figured he was in his late twenties or maybe thirty. His tanned, rough skin was due more to exposure than age. "Jessie, please." She shook his hand. "And this is Ki." Gil turned and shook hands with Ki. "He's my assistant and friend," Jessie said somewhat self-consciously. "Anything you'd say to me, you can say to him."

Gil nodded and said, "Fine." Then, somewhat puzzled, he added, "We were expecting you on the freight."

"There's been a slight accident," Jessie informed him.

As Jessie told the details, Ki studied Gil. There was something familiar about the man, something in the eyes. He noticed it first when they shook hands, but he did not let it trouble him; it would come back to him later.

When Gil had heard enough, he politely excused himself and called out instructions to a passing track layer. "Tinker, get Spike. Tell him the freight's been derailed at Bobcat Pass. I want a crew up there immediately. Then I want to see him here right quick." The track layer took off on the run.

A few moments of hectic activity passed. A flatbed crane

was wheeled out of the siding and coupled to a work train. Men laden with ropes, picks, and axes climbed into an empty boxcar. In the locomotive the fire was stoked, the boiler building up steam. When sufficient pressure was reached, the shrill *screech* of the whistle pierced the air. Men rushed aboard the train, and then as the engineer opened her up, the train rumbled down the line, leaving behind a trail of dense white smoke.

As Jessie turned from the sight, a brawny, barrel-chested man huffed up to the caboose. Gil introduced them. "Jessie and Ki, this is Spike McCaully, our foreman. Spike, Jessie Starbuck and Ki."

Spike nodded and said, "Damn air brakes! They ain't got the hold. They ain't safe for runnin' heavy loads."

"It wasn't the air brakes," interrupted Ki. "It was the timber barricading the tracks."

Spike thrust his meaty hand in Ki's face. "I don't know from no barricades, but three good brakemen would have kept her on the track!"

"I'm afraid Ki's right," added Jessie. "Three good brakemen would be three more dead bodies."

"I know all about bodies, ma'am. I started on the railroads a long time ago. There's a body for every mile of track laid. But this stuff that's happenin' now is just loco." Spike turned to Gil, "What're they doing here anyway?" he asked.

Gil answered calmly, "Commodore Whiting is a good friend of theirs."

"Ain't we got enough problems?"

Gil continued to calm the irate foreman. "Spike, they're here to help. Lord knows we need all the help we can get."

Spike refused to be appeased and practically ignored Gil's words. He turned instead to Jessie. "Damn! A railhead ain't no place for a woman."

Jessie had been studying the man. For all his anger, he showed little concern for the dead. Jessie could tell he was a belligerent man not used to being crossed. She did not usually choose to anger such types, but she found it necessary now to put him in his place. "Mr. McCaully, as a major stockholder in this railroad, my place is any damn place I choose!" she coolly informed him.

Spike spat on the ground and stormed off. As she watched him go, Jessie noticed that the Irishman's cheeks were burning red.

"Don't mind him," said Gil, a trace of a smile still clinging to his lips. "We usually don't see eye to eye either, but he means well."

"Is what he says true?" Jessie asked.

"Unfortunately, yes. A lot of lives go into building the railroads."

"No, I mean about the air brakes," Jessie explained.

The smile returned to Gil's face. "Depends on who you ask." He thought a moment and then continued, "For a railroad man Spike's old and conservative. Men like that get used to looking back, not ahead. Till now, brakemen with sticks would stop the trains. Every bend, every hill, every stop, they'd run from car to car manually setting the brakes with strong hickory sticks. Then they'd run back releasing 'em. There'd always be a grade, curve, or stop coming, so they stayed pretty busy. It worked, but it was inefficient." He let out a little chuckle. "Sometimes a train would stop a quarter of a mile past a depot and they'd have to back 'er up. It was dangerous work but—" He suddenly shrugged and then a bit apologetically added, "I'm getting a bit carried away."

Simultaneously, Jessie and Ki assured him of their interest. "Please go on," said Ki.

"It's fascinating," added Jessie. She was always intrigued by those who were not only consumed by their work, but were excited to share it with others.

Gil looked at them both and smiled rather boyishly. Jessie found the gesture charming. "Well, it's the same with coupling. Right now you lose a lot of fingers and a few lives, but you get the job done. In a few years there'll probably be automatic couplers on all the trains, but for now, well, the three-finger Ikes show their hands like a badge of courage." Gil took a deep breath. "I could go on, but to get to the point, I'm glad to be working for a man like Commodore Whiting. He looks to the future. That's why we're using heavier steel rails, not iron, and we're ballasting the roadbed. He's not afraid of technical advancements."

"He also cares about human life." added Jessie. It was a philosophy he shared with her father.

Gil nodded. "That's why we run air brakes. We're really building the railroad of the future," he said proudly. "In a few years the other roads will have to convert and rebuild, but we'll be set. Why don't I show you both around?"

"We'd like that," said Jessie.

"Good. It'll also give you an idea of what we're up against." They headed off to the lumberyard. "You know," Gil said chuckling, "forty years ago barges and wagons did the hauling and men like Spike McCaully were dead set against the railroads." They all grinned.

But by the time they made the rounds Jessie was no longer grinning. The tour was interesting and thorough, and she had learned even more about railroad construction. It left her all too keenly aware of how vulnerable they were, especially to sabotage. There were too many essential elements crucial to the construction that could be easily disrupted. A fire in the lumberyard, explosions, collisions, a collapse of a trestle—they would all be effective in slowing down the progress of the railroad. Even simply ripping up tracks would stall shipments of necessary raw materials. It was evident that more men were needed to guard against future mishaps.

She commented on this to Gil. He was very patient in his reply. "Every man we can get is put on the construction crew, and as it is, we're short."

"It's hard to figure a manpower shortage," Ki said.

"Not when certain word gets around." For emphasis, Gil lifted the sling that hung around his neck. "There's enough track being laid that a man figures he doesn't have to put up with a rail war in order to work."

"A few accidents are not a rail war," Jessie protested.

"It's enough to feed the rumors. When the risks seem too high, men just head for greener pastures," replied Gil. "Commodore Whiting's reputation's the only thing that's kept so many on."

Jessie had a feeling that Gil had something to do with keeping the crew together, but she kept it to herself. Pungent smoke was rising from the mess tent, reminding Jessie that they had not eaten since early morning. They had discussed enough business, and Jessie felt it wise to change the subject. "How's the chow?" she asked jovially.

"Plain but wholesome," was Gil's reply. He, too, seemed happy to change the subject. "Breakfast, though, is mighty good. "Pops'll rustle you up a stack of flapjacks that'll put a smile on the hungriest of grizzlies. But he doesn't do as well with the coffee," Gil added with a shrug.

As if on cue, the chow bell began to ring. Slowly men began laying down tools and heading for the mess tent. When Jessie, Ki, and Gil got there, Pops, the paunchy, gray-whiskered cook, stood patiently outside the tent. Gil introduced them.

"Why, Pops," Jessie said teasingly, "it looks like you should be out there laying tracks yourself."

The elderly cook beamed and straightened proudly. "Somebody has got to take care of the boys." He turned to Ki and eyed him closely. "A Chinaman? Part Chinaman? Sorry we ain't got no tea for you."

"Part Japanese. That's okay. I've heard lots about your coffee."

"Well, it's every bit as good as they say." Pops thought a moment and then gave Gil a dirty look. "They have been saying good things, ain't they?"

Gil jumped in and said, "There ain't a man here who'll bad-mouth your coffee, Pops. Least not to your face."

Pops passed over it and, turning back to Ki, said, "But I'll fix you up some chop suey that'll make you think you done died and gone to heaven. Learned it from Wo Hop when we was working the Central Pacific. Those were cold days, by golly, more'n a foot of snow fell before—"

"We'd love to hear it," Gil interrupted kindly, "but right now I want to get some hot food into our guests."

Pops turned back to the bell and spiritedly resumed hitting the metal triangle that hung from a wooden post. "Want my boys to get it while it's hot."

They sat and had dinner. Jessie found the food better than Gil's modest description. The coffee, though, was everything that he'd said. Just as they began to relax with some chitchat, a train whistle blew, and the work train, sent out earlier, came chugging back in. With a sigh, Gil got up and excused himself. But before he walked more than a few yards, a woman rushed into his arms. Jessie did not realize how much she had taken to Gil till a pang of jealousy slid through her. Jessie couldn't get a good look at the woman, for Gil was in her line of sight, but she heard the conversation clear enough.

"When I heard you were hurt, I was worried. I had to come out and see for myself," the woman said.

"I can take care of myself. You know that, Cynth," Gil stated flatly.

They began walking back to where Jessie was. "This time, but how 'bout the next?" As they got closer, Jessie recognized the woman as the one whom Ki had rescued. She noted, though, that now the woman's torn dress was pinned up. The woman continued, "Why can't you get a safe job back home, Gil?"

"Because my job is building railroads," Gil said.

"Then why not another railroad, one where I won't have to worry about you getting shot at and killed."

"No one's doing any shooting. And I finish what I start!" His tone was definite; he was not going to discuss the matter further.

"And maybe someone else also wants to finish what he started!" she countered, indicating the sling around his neck.

Gil ignored her comment, and as they reached his seat, he turned to Jessie. Cynthia kept talking. "Why must you be so pigheaded."

Just then, Ki looked up from his plate. Cynthia's surprise and delight couldn't keep from showing. Her tone changed immediately. "But if you're gonna be stubborn, I'd better stick around and look after your well-being."

"You'll do no such thing," Gil snapped.

"I can be as mulish as you, Gil Johnson, maybe even more so."

"This is no place for you, Cynthia," Gil shot back at her.

Cynthia folded her arms across her chest and looked away. Case closed! Jessie let out a chuckle; she liked Cynthia's spunk.

"Damn! A railhead is no place for a woman," continued Gil. His words fell on deaf ears. He started to protest more, but when he caught sight of Jessie giving him a dirty look, he stopped abruptly. "I guess I'm sounding an awful lot like Spike now, huh," he said sheepishly. Jessie smiled and nodded. With a loud sigh, Gil admitted defeat.

"Jessie, this is my sister, Cynthia. Sometimes she sounds an awful lot like my mother." Turning to Cynthia, who was already smiling victoriously, Gil continued. "Sis, this is Jessie Starbuck and Ki."

"My pleasure," said Cynthia. It was more than a simple courtesy; her words seemed to have a special meaning as she stared into Ki's eyes. "We've already met," she said to her brother, "though we haven't been formally introduced."

A sudden loud explosion interrupted further conversation. One of the equipment shacks was blown to bits, and thick rolling clouds of black smoke were curling to the sky.

★

Chapter 3

"The nitro!" screamed Gil. He joined the crowd of men running to the exploded shack, but he quickly changed his mind. He grabbed the man on his right, "Jensen, quick, the TNT!" The two men started running the other way, but were knocked flat by a second, even louder explosion. The second blast caused more commotion. Men racing to the scene of the first accident now stopped short, unsure which way to head. Others were bumping into one another in their hurry to get to either one of the sites. Meanwhile, the remains of the first shack had flared up, and containing the fire seemed of paramount importance. But timbers from the second detonation also threatened to burst into flames, and men had to be divided between the two areas. As testimony to the experience of the workers, the commotion was soon replaced by well-organized crews. Ditches were quickly dug around the burning structures, and dirt was being thrown on the smoldering remains. In a relatively short time, things were under control.

At the sound of the second explosion, Jessie and Ki had

exchanged glances. If they were in doubt after the first blast, there was no longer any question. Two buildings, a hundred yards apart, don't both spontaneously go up in a matter of moments. It was sabotage.

Jessie leaned toward Ki, but she almost had to shout to be heard above the noise. "I'm going to stay here with Cynthia, but you take a look around for anything suspicious."

Ki nodded and was off. He avoided, as best he could, the efforts of the firefighters. Slowly and nonchalantly, he circled one devastated building. The destruction was such that he didn't expect to find any damning evidence like a kerosene lamp, oil can, or detonator cap. In fact, none was necessary. It wouldn't take much more than a lit cigar and a length of fuse to set off a storage shack full of explosives. But to Ki's trained eye, what he did not find was important. He didn't find any telltale horse tracks, a sure sign that the saboteur could not have gotten far.

Ki slowly walked from the center of activity and began to scan the perimeter of the camp carefully. He spotted a man heading toward the lumberyard, and although that in itself did not make him the culprit, to be walking away from everything at a time when all others are involved in frantic salvage activity was highly suspicious. Ki took off after him.

Ki was quick and silent, but there was a lot of distance to cover, and as guilty men are wont to do, the suspected saboteur nervously glanced over his shoulder before he was about to duck into the lumberyard. He spotted Ki and drew his gun. Ki continued running at full speed, but as he saw the man level his gun, he dropped into a forward somersault. The bullet whizzed over his head. The second shot also went by harmlessly. To an observer, Ki's pursuit would have seemed like a very risky gamble or utter foolishness. For Ki, it was neither. Western opponents were not used to such acrobatics. A gunman would aim at his target and fire. An unarmed man would be considered a dead duck. But with his mastery of martial arts, Ki was anything but unarmed. A forward tumble took Ki out of the line of fire. And a gunman would fire where his target was, not where his target might move to.

When Ki nimbly rose to his feet, he was that much closer to the startled man. After missing Ki with two shots, the man panicked and fled. Ki was upon him quickly. The suspect turned, hoping for one last shot. But an accurately delivered *mae-tobi-geri,* a forward flying kick, to the man's arm sent the gun sailing into the air. It would be fairly simple to overpower the man. Ki made a mental note to work on the man's torso and stay away from vital spots like the neck and bridge of the nose. Not only should the man be taken alive, but conscious as well. An unconscious captive could not tell of an immediate rendezvous with other cohorts. It would be wiser to work the body with a series of snapping kicks to the sides. A man could survive with any number of broken ribs.

The first kick sent the man tumbling backward, and as he came up, a six-inch bowie knife flashed in his hand. No matter. Ki watched the wrist carefully, but continued pummeling the man's body with powerful kicks. Ki's foot could make contact and return before the knife could be brought to bear. He kept his opponent confused and off balance, wondering where he would kick next. But on his fourth kick a lucky slash caught him high on the thigh, the sharp blade ripping into his pants. Better to deal with the knife now and not worry about another lucky and possibly deadly thrust. Ki now shifted his total attention to his opponent's wrist. He gave his adversary a moment to catch his breath. The best way to dispense with the knife would be to render the knife-wielding arm useless. After a few feints the man lunged, and as Ki suspected he might, the man overextended himself. Ki sidestepped neatly and grabbed hold of the wrist as the knife went past. His other hand delivered a quick, powerful strike to the forearm. With the force of the blow and his firm lock on the wrist, something had to give—the radius cracked sharply; the knife dropped to the ground. The man let out a painful shriek and then was suddenly silent as he dropped to the ground. Only then did Ki become aware of a gunshot, hearing the last echo as it faded swiftly into the air. Looking down at his opponent, he saw the red spread across the dead man's chest. He let go of the lifeless wrist.

A crowd was gathering a few yards away, alerted by the first shots fired at Ki, early in the chase. At the center Spike McCaully was holstering his Colt. Jessie rushed to him. "You might have shot Ki," she said furiously.

Halfheartedly, Spike defended himself. "The man had a knife, and"—gesturing to Ki—"he was unarmed."

Jessie suppressed a chuckle. "Ki can take care of himself."

Cynthia rushed to Ki. She was the first to notice the blood stain on his pants. "You're bleeding!" she exclaimed. Even Ki had not realized till then that the slash had drawn blood.

"It's not serious," Ki replied.

"Serious or not, I want to have a look at it and, if nothing else, wash it."

"I've had worse," Ki said matter-of-factly.

"I'll have none of your modesty; now get." Cynthia was having the last word.

Gil instructed two men to give Ki a hand, but Ki turned down their assistance. He assured everyone he was quite capable of walking by himself. Cynthia, though, came alongside him and draped his arm around her shoulder. It offered little help; she was not able to shoulder much of Ki's weight, but Ki found his hand resting pleasantly over her right breast. As his palm brushed against her, he felt her nipple stiffen. The anger that Ki felt because the saboteur, their only lead, was shot dead was soon replaced by other more pleasing thoughts. But before Ki turned totally to the more arousing aspects of the situation, he became aware of the distinct possibility that Spike's bullet might have missed its intended target. It would have been difficult for someone to have gotten a clear shot. As he sidestepped his assailant's knife, he might also have dodged a bullet meant for himself. He would have time to ponder that later. Right now Cynthia's soft voice was cooing in his ear. "I'll take you into the caboose and fix you right up," she said warmly.

The caboose served as both office and bedroom and was furnished with a drafting board, bookshelves, and bed. Once in Gil's private car, Cynthia got right to work. She sat Ki in a chair and then said, "I can cut the leg off or you can slip out of 'em." She was, of course, referring to Ki's pants. Without a word he slid out of his jeans. If she was aware that he wore no underclothes, she made no notice of it. His loose-fitting, cotton shirt covered his manhood, but his growing erection caused his shirt to tent out conspicuously. Still, she knelt on the floor and tended to his wound, a three-inch gash halfway up the outer side of his thigh.

They had first stopped by the mess tent to pick up a pan of hot water, and Cynthia was using her kerchief to wash away the caked blood. She then opened a bottle of whiskey and splashed some on the kerchief. "This might sting some, but it's necessary." Ki's leg jerked slightly. He could have focused his concentration elsewhere and been completely unaffected by the stinging medication, but for some perverse reason, he chose not to. Cynthia lowered her lips to his thigh and kissed his wound tenderly. "I'm sorry," she said softly. Her hair felt good against his inner thigh. "I think I'll leave it open. It's clean and the air will do it good." She kissed it lightly.

"That's why many animals lick their wounds," Ki said.

"Like this?" Cynthia began to lick the inside of his thigh. She moved her way up slowly—till her breath was warm against his crotch. With her free hand, she began to slide Ki's shirt up over his erection. Her tongue traveled upon every bit of exposed flesh, and soon she was licking the entire length of his rock-hard shaft. She would flatten her tongue and run it up one side; then using only the tip of her tongue she would lightly run it down the other. Ki reached out, took hold of her head, and guided it to his pulsing organ. As her hungry mouth took him in, Ki let out a moan.

Cynthia quickly pulled away and looked at his leg. "I didn't hurt you, did I?" Ki shook his head. "I was afraid I might have put too much weight on it," she said and then lowered her head once more.

Ki felt her begin sucking, the pressure within him building slowly with each move of her head. As she held him in her mouth, her tongue began doing a dance of its own along Ki's most sensitive skin. Colors flickered across Ki's closed eyes. He began to move his hips, slowly at first and then with increasing speed. He twined his fingers into her hair and began pumping deep into her throat, her teeth scraping against his base. Whether this went on for an eternity or only a short moment, Ki was unaware. He was disassociated from his body, lost in a fog of sensual pleasure. Eventually Cynthia pulled away from his throbbing pole. "Relax; I don't want you to exert yourself. You might open up that cut," she said, catching her breath and swallowing. Her actions, though, were designed for anything but relaxation. With both hands she continued to stroke his shaft—lightly and quickly; then slowly and firmly. "You're as red as a beet." She squeezed rapidly with her fingers. "And I bet as sweet." She took a tentative lick of his crimson shaft and then lowered her mouth over it. As her warm lips engulfed him, Ki felt a tremor pass through him. Against the back of her throat, his floodgates opened. He spasmed violently against the roof of her mouth twice and then was still. Cynthia slowly drew back her head. Her big brown eyes were smiling. "Now, I want you to rest," she said soothingly as she helped him into the bed. "You've lost a lot of blood and other fluid." Ki did not protest, as he put his head down against the pillow.

• • •

The workers were not as content as Ki. That this latest incident was blatant sabotage did not escape them. But what irked them more was the identity of the saboteur. Had he been an unknown thug, things would have been different, but he was a fellow tracklayer, hired just a few weeks ago. If one saboteur had infiltrated their midst, there might be others.

A large group of men had gathered outside the mess tent to discuss their course of action. As soon as he realized what was going on, Gil quickly hurried over. He was now standing on a long wooden table addressing the crowd. "Most of you men are angry and some are confused, just like I am, but I do know one thing, and that's that we all signed on to build a railroad."

"Y'can't build without dynamite," someone shouted from the back of the crowd. There were other shouts of support.

Gil held up his hands to quiet them. "We got another two days of track to lay before we need more explosives. By then another shipment will have arrived."

"What'n hell'll happen by then, I ask you?" shouted another voice from the crowd.

"How many more'll have to kick the bucket?" added another. The crowd was getting riled up and unruly.

"There were only some minor burns. No one died," Gil said emphatically. "You men know the risks; there are always lives lost."

"But not caused by our own. That fella worked with us, slept with us, drank with us," said a familiar voice. "Is the man workin' by your side gonna do you in at night?"

Dissenting comments came from different spots in the crowd, but there started to be a repetition of voices. Jessie began to suspect the presence of agitators among the workers and, from her position alongside the table, began to search for the frequent speakers.

"There's better fishin' on the other side of the stream," said the first man. Others were quick to agree, and it was only moments before the inevitable.

"I'm pulling my freight and headin' to the Great Northern." The dissent spread like wildfire through the crowd. It was obvious to Jessie they had reached a critical point.

It was also very evident to Gil. "Hold it! Hold it! Everybody just set your brakes," he said quickly. "I've known most of you a fair spell now, and I know you're good, honest men." He would have to talk fast and he knew it. "When the yard was burnin' back in Lodgepole, we all blackened our faces and burned our lungs fighting the blaze. And when Jake and his crew were caught in the cave-in, there wasn't a man here didn't pick up shovel and dig till he dropped. I didn't hear complaints then! Well, we pulled together and we saved a few." He could feel the crowd swaying to his side. "We all owe our lives to whoever's standin' next to us. If he didn't save you yesterday, he sure will tomorrow." Gil took a deep breath. "Now, Jake ain't with us, but I sure know what he'd say. He'd tell you he's a railroad man and he signed on to lay tracks. And if we quit before we get to the Pacific, then Jake and the others, well, they just died for nothing."

Gil stopped and was quiet. He believed what he said and felt that most of his men did, too. There was nothing more he could say or do. The men were silent, all deep in their own thoughts. Gil had taken an unruly mob and turned them into thoughtful individuals. Jessie also found herself moved by Gil's spirited words, and she waited expectantly.

Eventually a soft voice called out, "We're with you, Gil. What can we do?"

His sentiments were echoed by another. "Yeah, we can't let them run us off."

Gil feared if he didn't have a good answer he might lose them once again. He looked to Jessie, hesitated, then turned back to the crowd. "Some of you might be wondering who that new man is and what he's doing here. Well, his name is Ki, and he's a Pinkerton." A murmur went through the crowd. "He's had a lot of experience with these things," continued Gil. "He's busted mining gangs in the East and he's worked with other roads. He's a good man to have. He hasn't been here a day and he's already caught one. He'll have our problem licked in no time." It seemed best to say no more, so Gil stepped down off the table and walked off.

He went to Jessie. "I hope you don't mind what I said about Ki?" he asked.

Jessie shook her head. "You said what had to be said. And anyway, it isn't so far from the truth."

"No, I guess it isn't." Gil seemed relieved to have her approval. "I do think Ki's a good man and I'm mighty glad you're here, Jessie."

"Why, thank you, Gil. I just wish it weren't dirty business that brought us here." The sun had already set and the first stars were just beginning to twinkle in the twilight sky. The air was cool and a gentle breeze rustled the tops of the trees. Tranquility had finally come to a hectic and violent day, but at the mention of business Gil's brow became deeply furrowed. Jessie brushed a lock of his curly hair off his forehead. "Don't worry, Gil, the cartel hasn't beaten me yet. I don't intend to let them start now."

"The cartel?"

"I think they're the ones who are behind this," Jessie informed him.

"Well, then, what's stopping us from rounding them up?"

Jessie smiled. "If it were only that easy!" Just then Ki approached them. He favored his injured leg slightly, but other than that he seemed fine. Jessie turned to him with a smile. "Feeling okay?"

"Fine." Ki nodded.

"Are you sure you should be walking?" Gil asked.

"Your sister has a nice healing hand. I'm as good as new, maybe a sight better," he said, smiling.

Jessie wanted to give Ki a playful shove, for she had a good idea what Ki really meant by that, but considering Gil, she let it pass.

"Well, it's getting late for us railroad folk—" Gil started to say.

"For all of us," Jessie piped in.

"I've had two tents pitched over by the tool shed for you and Ki," Gil told them. "If you need anything, I've moved into the mess tent temporarily." He nodded to Ki, but let his eyes linger on Jessie briefly before bidding good night.

★

Chapter 4

Jessie pushed back the flap of her tent and stepped out of the night. As expected, the tent was plain and simple, but most important, it offered some semblance of privacy. At the center it was roomy enough to stand in, and it was furnished with a narrow cot. On the cot were a clean bedroll and Jessie's leather saddlebag. On the ground there was a basin of water. Jessie smiled at Gil's thoughtfulness. Now that he had popped into her mind, she let her thoughts dwell on him. She respected the way he handled his men. There was something she liked about him right from the start. He had an engaging smile. Just thinking about it brought a smile to her face and made her want to tousle his curly hair. But there was more to it than looks. It was, she realized, his sincerity. He believed in his work, in the railroad, and in himself. It was his strong sense of conviction and purpose that made him so attractive. Of course, his smile didn't hurt, she added to herself.

Thinking of purpose, though, brought her back around to matters at hand. She opened her bag and dug out a small, black leather diary from the bottom. This book was a copy of a larger ledger that was safely locked in a secret drawer of her father's desk. Every time she opened the book she could almost smell the cherry scent of her father's pipe tobacco. She held the book up to her nose and smiled. There was a faint trace of it.

While sitting on the cot, she leaned forward and turned up the wick of the kerosene lamp that hung from the center pole of the tent. The book contained a list, initially kept by her father, of all the known cartel agents whom he had discovered. Since his death, Jessie had added quite a few names uncovered during her own investigations. To an observer not familiar with the code the book was written in, it would all seem like senseless jibberish. But the book had proved invaluable throughout her fight with the cartel.

She now flipped the pages searching for any name that she might connect with sabotage. She noted that Spike McCaully was not listed, though that meant nothing. It was neither a sign of innocence nor guilt. The cartel was constantly expanding, always feeding its ranks with the corrupt and dishonest. And it was unfortunate that here in the West, a land of rich opportunity, greedy and evil men were none too scarce.

She extinguished the lamp and lay on the cot, but she could not fall asleep. She wondered how to turn the tables on the cartel, how to get the upper hand on an unseen adversary. But she could come up with no easy answer. With time and perhaps her share of luck, things would change. Ki had once told her, "Things are forever changing; one has just to remain still long enough to perceive it." Well, she would wait, she told herself.

Trying to relax, she began to think once more of Gil. But the cartel intruded and her last thoughts were not pleasant. She dearly hoped no harm would come to Gil.

In his tent, Ki also found it difficult to sleep. It was not the throbbing of his leg that bothered him, but a restless, active mind. His thoughts, though, had nothing to do with the cartel. They had to do with big brown eyes and flowing curls of brown hair. Now as he closed his eyes, sleep seemed to elude him. In its place, he saw visions of Cynthia. He felt her breath and her warmth pressing against him. His mind focused on particular moments with Cynthia: her breasts pressing against him that morning on the train, his hands lightly brushing her nipples as she helped him to the caboose, and then, of course, the warmth of her mouth. He recalled the heat in his loins and was not surprised to find himself fully aroused, his manhood pressed against his pants. He knew sleep would be futile, so he got up and went outside.

There was a crescent moon hanging just above the tree line, and with no clouds in the sky, that little sliver lit up the night sky. The sky was also ablaze with hundreds of stars. Ki knew something of the constellations; on his voyage to America, he had been taught to navigate by the stars. But it took him a while to orient himself to being this far north. After a moment he was absorbed looking for groupings that were not visible down at the Circle Star. The stars above his head and the cool earth against his bare feet gave him a deep sense of tranquility. But he caught his breath when he noticed a faint glow of a kerosene lamp coming from Gil's caboose.

He felt a strange excitement as he climbed the steps of the caboose. The iron rungs were cold against his feet. Every sense within him seemed to be working at a higher level; he was keenly aware of everything. As he silently opened the door, he quickly took in the whole scene: Gil's stack of books on the wall, the chart opened on the drafting table, and on the bed, cast in the soft, warm glow of the lamp, Cynthia stretched languidly, her nightdress pulled up past her naked hips. Her hands covered her soft bush, but wisps of curly brown hair poked out between the fingers. Her hands moved in a slow circular pattern; then one finger disappeared. Cynthia's eyes were closed and she let out a soft moan. She remained like that for a moment and then withdrew her hand. Ki could see the moist dew on her pink petals. She let out a sigh and began to rock her hips. She began to smile slightly, wistfully, and then stretched out her legs to their full length.

Throughout it all, Ki remained standing silently. A moment later Ki took a quick and noiseless step to the bed. He slipped out of his clothes. Her eyes flickered. Grabbing her, he lowered himself onto and then into her.

"Oh, Ki, yes!" she sighed loudly. Ki pressed his lips to hers, his tongue darting hungrily inside her mouth. Her warm tunnel engulfed his manhood. He began to pump into her with a fury. She met his every thrust, her body lifting off the bed to do so. Her nails raked Ki's back, urging him on to even greater passion. His thrusts were just as deep and their speed increased. Cynthia began a moan from deep within. She drew her legs up and locked them around Ki's waist; her hands grabbed for his smooth rump and pushed him deeper into her. She pressed against him, grinding tightly. Ki felt her first shudder, then arched his muscular back, and rammed his full length into her. On his next stroke, Ki exploded deep inside her. Cynthia's shaking began again, her whole body trembling for a full minute.

"I've been thinking of you all night," she whispered into his ear. "But I never imagined it like this," she added with a smile.

"I couldn't sleep. I was thinking about you," confessed Ki. His head was resting against her bosom. With his hand he undid the bodice ties and freed her swollen breasts. He kneaded her one breast in his powerful hand and traced her dark nipple with his tongue. "Since this morning, I've been thinking about this. I wanted you on the train," he said between licks.

"You should have taken me," she said and laughed. "I was yours for the asking."

He responded by sucking her hard bud into his mouth.

Cynthia ran her hands through his black hair. Still inside her, Ki began to rock gently.

"You're as hard as before," Cynthia said in amazement. But her surprise soon turned to joy. She lifted Ki off her slightly and slid out from under him. She rolled and then got up on all fours. She turned her head and said hungrily, "Take me."

Ki kneeled, grabbed her around the hips, and plunged into her. He thrust slowly, feeling every inch of her swallow his rigid rod. He'd penetrate her to the hilt, and then pull her even closer to him.

"Oh, so deep!" cooed Cynthia. Her body began to sway from side to side—her soft bottom moving one way, her pendulous breasts swinging the other. Ki stretched out his arms and cupped her large globes in his hands. He massaged them firmly, and the pointed tips were soon pressing into the palms of his hands. Impaled firmly on Ki's dagger, Cynthia began to arch her back and tilt her pelvis—slowly at first, then with an increasing passion. He began pumping her harder.

"Yes! Yes!" she began to scream. Her body began to jerk spasmodically, her breasts heaving. Her breath came in short gasps. Ki continued to ride her. "You have to stop," she began to plead, "Oh, but not yet, not yet." Ki continued with rapid, powerful thrusts. "I can't believe . . . not again!" she cried.

"Tell me when." Words were not necessary. Her body began to convulse. Cynthia buried her head into the pillow and let go with a muffled scream. Her throaty yell and the tight grip she had on his swelling tool urged him on to his own ecstasy. Her fingers clutched the pillow and another tremor wracked her quivering body. At the same instant, Ki let go inside her, and they both collapsed onto her bed.

They lay now side by side, Cynthia's breathing slowly returning to normal. The kerosene in the lamp had been depleted and the moonlight shining through the windows of the caboose replaced the soft glow of the lamp. Ki's eyes glanced over Cynthia's curves. The warm tones of flesh afire were now the cool glaze of naked marble.

Cynthia was fast asleep and Ki had drifted off into a light, peaceful slumber. He was unsure how long he dozed, but at the sound of galloping horses he bolted upright, instantly alert. He slipped into his pants and rushed out quickly. Then he saw and heard flames.

There was no immediate danger. Had he been in his tent, though, it would have been a totally different story. He turned his attention away from the flames and focused on a rapidly retreating rider. There was no hope of successful pursuit, but he listened intently for the number of horses and the direction they were heading. As he stood there, it literally hit him—the breeze. He was foolish not to have realized it at first, but there was no time for self-recrimination. He ran at full speed to Jessie's tent. He had thought there was no danger and no reason not to let his tent burn safely to the ground. But with a stiff wind blowing, his burning tent could easily become a dangerous torch, capable of igniting Jessie's tent pitched not ten yards away.

With a *whoosh* his blazing tent toppled on its side. Ki surged forward, forcing his legs into longer, faster strides. There still might be time. A gust of wind shot fingers of flame along the ground. For a brief instant fire licked at the base of Jessie's tent and then with a bright roar engulfed the tent in a mass of fire. The dry canvas would burn quickly, but there was another danger besides the fire. To repel water, the tents were coated with a film of oil and grease. Black acrid smoke swirled around the tent. Jessie was in immediate danger of asphyxiation.

Ki covered the last few yards in seconds and, taking a deep breath, burst into the tent. The interior was fast filling with smoke. Jessie was slumped, half off the bed. She probably woke as the tent caught fire, but was quickly overcome by the noxious fumes and smoke. Ki wrapped her in a blanket and scooped her into his arms. After covering her as best he could, he rushed out of the deadly inferno into the cool night air.

"Fire!" someone yelled. The camp was quickly springing to life. Men were rushing to the scene, eager to help, but there was little that needed doing now.

Once out of the tent, Jessie was revived quickly. Ki laid her on the ground and splashed some fresh water on her face. That was all that was needed to bring her around. After a brief coughing spell, she opened her eyes.

"Good morning," Ki said, genuinely relieved.

"Ki, what happened?" Jessie seemed confused and disoriented.

"There was a fire and you inhaled some smoke."

Jessie looked around. "An accident?" It wasn't really a question, but Ki shook his head anyway. "And you pulled me out?" This time Ki nodded.

Gil came running up and dropped to his knees beside Jessie. "Are you okay?" he asked breathlessly.

"Yes, I'm fine, Gil."

"Thank goodness!" Gil sighed with relief. "What happened?" he asked Ki.

"Someone set fire to my tent and the wind spread the fire to Jessie's tent."

"Did you see anything?"

"Only that they got away on horses."

"Damn!" Gil rose to his feet angrily.

The remains of the tents had been doused with water and Spike was dispersing the men. "All right lads, back to your tents. It's all done—only a lamp fire. Let it be a lesson to you to mind your lamps."

The men started heading back to their beds, but one stopped by Ki and gave him a brotherly pat on the back. "They're scared of ya, Ki. They know what ya can do."

"But we're with ya, every step of the way," added his companion.

"What was that about?" Ki wondered out loud after they had gone.

"I'm afraid that was my fault, Ki," Gil said apologetically. "This whole incident may be due to my stupidity."

"Don't blame yourself," Jessie said.

"Who else is there to blame?" Gil asked.

"The man who held the match," offered Ki.

Gil turned to Ki. "I owe you an apology—and an explanation. Earlier I was in a fix so I told the men you were a Pinkerton. I told 'em you had cracked tougher cases and you'd crack this one, too!"

"In a sense you weren't lying," Ki said matter-of-factly.

"But it was responsible for this. They tried to do you in."

"Every time the cartel exposes its hand there's the chance for us to chop it off," Ki offered.

"I just don't want anything to happen to either of you."

"Or at least nothing that a good scrubbing won't fix." Cynthia had just joined them, and until her comment, neither Jessie nor Ki realizied how covered with soot and smoke they both were. "Don't just sit there, Gil; get us some warm water," she said.

As Gil started to leave, Jessie got to her feet. "I think I'll come with you; I could do with a cup of coffee."

"There should be a bottle around, too. I could do with a shot of whiskey. How 'bout you, Ki?" Gil asked.

"Sounds like what the doctor ordered," Ki said amiably.

As they walked to the mess tent, Cynthia took hold of Ki's hands and inspected him for burns. "You're just singed. The doctor'll recommend a good cleanin' and some tender care," she said softly.

"I don't think I have enough energy for your kind of care," answered Ki with a sly grin.

Over drinks they became good friends, momentarily forgetting the bleak events that had brought them together in the first place. They discussed the relevant issues and reminisced. Ki even talked a little about Japan, something he would not do often. At one point their laughter woke the sleepy-eyed cook.

Pops staggered out from his bed, cussin' the whole way. "This ain't no church social. A man can't get no shuteye 'round here," he groused.

Reluctantly Gil realized the time. "There are still a few hours to mornin'." Looking to Jessie, he continued, "Why don't you go to the caboose with Cynth, and Ki can bed down in here with me?"

"As soon as it's light, I'd like to try to pick up their trail. If I can get a horse—" Ki started to say.

"Make that two," Jessie finished.

Gil thought a moment. "I have some surveying to do. Why don't we all head out together?"

Everyone but Cynthia liked the idea. But she was smart enough to know when she would be in the way. "I reckon I'll keep Pops company."

"Maybe you could teach him a thing or two about coffee," Gil suggested.

★

Chapter 5

The camp was just beginning to stir as Jessie, Ki, and Gil picked their way up the heavily wooded slope that lay along the southern side of the railroad tracks. Behind them, wisps of smoke rose from the mess tent and the smell of frying bacon drifted slowly in the air. Pops had wanted them to stay for breakfast, but they were eager to hit the trail as soon as possible. Calling them impetuous, Pops filled their saddlebags with biscuits, beans, dried beef, a slab of bacon, and a small sack of chicory coffee.

So far, things were going well. The escaping arsonists seemed more concerned with speed than stealth and left an easily followed trail in the dirt of the forest floor. Ki, in the lead, only had to dismount once to find the trail. Otherwise, he led his dark brown quarter horse steadily onward. Following close behind, Jessie and Gil rode side by side. Jessie was riding a small but spirited roan. Gil couldn't help admire the way Jessie's body swayed gracefully with the movement of the horse, the way her long legs wrapped firmly around the belly of the animal. After a number of feeble attempts and false starts, Gil finally commented on this.

"You make a pretty couple—you and the horse," he added quickly to clarify himself, "especially when the sun shines through the trees."

"Thank you, Gil." She patted the horse's mane, accepting the compliment for the animal as well. "She's a good one, but I miss Sun."

Gil shot her an inquisitive look. It was now Jessie's turn to explain. "Sun is my horse back home on the Circle Star. She's a beautiful golden palomino and smart . . ." Her tone was full of motherly pride. "Folks who know her swear she understands English."

"Well does she?"

"If she doesn't, she ain't saying," Jessie teased him playfully. "But we do have a real understanding for each other," she added seriously. "She's gotten me out of more than one scrape. But listen to me, I sound like a doting mother."

Gil smiled and Jessie felt more than the rays of the morning sun warming her. Gil sat upright and looked very much at ease atop his gray stallion. Even riding at a slow pace, there was something in his posture that told of an experienced horseman. His hands held the reins loosely, almost casually, but it was evident that Gil was in full control. Jessie could sense the power that lay behind the light touch.

"You ride well." Then, a bit self-conscious, she added playfully, "For an Easterner."

"Thank you, I think. But what makes you say that I'm an Easterner?"

"Well, are you?"

Gil sounded defensive. "I was born in Missouri, but when my father died, my mom moved the family back to the East."

Jessie felt she had hit a sore spot. "It's not so much your mannerisms as your education. You're the railroad's locator. Most locators and chief surveyors don't learn their trade in the hills. It's usually at some school in the East."

Gil's grin grew even bigger. "Yale, to be precise," he

said with much feigned self-importance.

"Why, sir, I am duly impressed," she said with an equal flourish. "So then how does a nice young man from New Haven learn to ride so well?"

"You know, most women west of the Mississippi haven't heard of Yale. Even fewer know it's in New Haven." As soon as it was said, he was instantly sorry.

"We're not all born with hay between our teeth, Mr. Johnson," she said with a shake of her head and then turned to face forward. Even she was surprised by the icy tone of her voice. Well, if he thinks his upbringing is so damn special... she thought to herself. Without finishing her thought, she urged her horse a step or two ahead of his. Watching her tawny mane catch the light, Gil was even sorrier for his inadvertent slip.

Jessie reined in next to Ki, who was waiting up ahead. "I have a feeling our luck has just run out," he said, pointing straight ahead. Through the trees there was a narrow band of shimmering iridescence and the faint sound of rushing waters could be heard.

Though the stream turned out to be narrow, it proved sufficient to wipe away any trace of the arsonists' route. Sunlight peeked through the thick pine boughs and danced across the frothy, gurgling water. As the wind stirred the trees, patterns of shimmering light rippled fancifully and added to the effervescence of the cool spring. All along its length, the swirling water sparkled like so many jewels. In any other situation it would have been a beautiful sight, but now it signaled the end of the trail.

When Gil caught up to Jessie and Ki, he found both riders waiting by the bank, looking very disappointed. "I reckon this means we've lost them," he said to no one in particular.

"We could search both sides of the bank, but I don't think we'll pick up the trail," Ki said as he leaned back in his saddle. "It also explains why the signs were so easy to read."

"Why?" Gil asked innocently.

"Because, professor," Jessie began impatiently, "they knew we'd lose them in the stream. They didn't have to worry about us being on their tail."

"Well, that tells us the weasels know the lay of the land," Gil added enthusiastically.

Jessie seemed unimpressed by Gil's insight and shrugged.

"He's right," Ki added with a smile. "And that might come in helpful later on. Anyway, there's still a fifty-fifty chance we'll turn up something." He turned to Gil, "Which way do you need to go?"

Gil checked his pocket compass and then pointed downstream. "Just about southwest from here."

"Downstream for us, then." Ki reined his horse about. "Why don't you stay on this side, Jessie, and I'll take the left? We still might pick up some sign."

Gil edged his horse behind Jessie's. "Why don't I ride with you?" he started to say, but stopped abruptly when he caught sight of Jessie's leer.

"Why don't you ride in the middle of the stream?" Jessie snapped. "That way we'll have everything covered."

Hoping for support, sympathy, or encouragement, Gil looked to Ki. But Ki thought it best not to say anything; he could barely suppress the grin that threatened to break out across his calm features. So with a rider on either bank and Gil wading through the middle, they began their trek downstream. Gil let the horse pick its own way through the water, and occasionally the horse would step down into a pool and dunk Gil up to the shin. Jessie watched from the bank as Gil got both legs thoroughly wet. As he dipped into another pool, she took mercy and called out to him. "You keep doing that and you're liable to be cooling your bottom and looking up at the sky—if your horse doesn't throw a shoe first."

"Mighty glad for the invite, Miss Starbuck," Gil replied and then led his horse up the bank. "It's my feet that are wet, but I'm glad to see you've cooled off some."

"I guess they didn't teach you everything at that university, Mr. Johnson, or you'd know that women in general and Texans in specific don't like to be mocked. And the sooner you learn..."

Gil slowly lowered his head and formally tipped his Stetson. When he looked back at Jessie, he had a huge smile.

Jessie quickly changed her tone. "Maybe you're not as dumb as you seem." That damn smile, she thought to herself.

Gradually the stream began to cut deeper into the land and the soft earthy banks gave way to hard granite. Large boulders rose from the water's edge, raising the banks a good ten feet. Ki led his horse down one of the more gently sloping rocks, crossed the stream, and climbed up to join Jessie and Gil. "Even if they came this way, we'll never catch a print on this rock," he said as he pulled in alongside them.

"Well, if it happens again, we won't let 'em get this far," Gil said optimistically.

"Unfortunately, it will happen again and again—until we stop them or they stop us." There was no bitterness in Jessie's voice, just a weary knowledge that every battle with the cartel was to the finish.

"Well, they're not going to stop me, and I don't intend to let anybody stop the railroad."

"If we want to win," Jessie said, smiling, "it's going to take just that kind of thinking."

Encouraged by Jessie, Gil broke out into a smile as well. "And I don't plan to stop till I see those blue waters of the Pacific."

"Then let's get back to work," Jessie said resolutely. "We have a railroad coming through! Gil, about your surveying..."

Gil unrolled a chart from its case and studied it a minute. "Seems like the best way is just to follow this stream. There's a pass about seven miles from here I want to give a second look to." He continued to inspect his chart and, without looking up, added, "But that might be none too easy. The elevation rises pretty quickly."

Ki let out a small chuckle. "You don't need a lit tinder to know which way the wind blows." Gil looked at him questioningly. "You can get a good sense of that by just looking," explained Ki, as he pointed to the mountain slope just off in the distance.

"We could wade through the stream," Gil suggested. "The water's not deep and, after the initial shock, not really that cold."

It was no sooner said than done. The water not only proved to be shallow, but in many places high sand bars, covered by only a few inches of water, made for easy travel. Away from the edges, though, the current continued to move strong and fast, and the banks grew steeper as the land began to tower above both sides of the stream. Within two miles the water was cutting a deep gorge through solid rock. It was early in the afternoon, but the sun was just beginning to dip behind the canyon walls, spreading shadows across the face of the stream.

Jessie voiced her concern quietly to Ki. "What do you think?"

"I suppose we can always backtrack. There's still plenty of time for that, but I don't have a good feeling about this."

Jessie nodded. It might have been the gloom caused by the long shadows or the eerie echoes trapped by the canyon walls, but she felt it as well. Though you didn't always understand, you learned to heed that inner voice. It might be sensing a copperhead, coiled and ready to strike, a flash storm coming out of nowhere, or a twister growing across an open plain. In the wilds, survival often took more than knowledge; it took what many called prairie luck, though it was anything but. Sometimes it was just giving the elements their due respect, and sometimes it was knowing what to do when the hairs on the back of the neck started to rise.

Jessie turned to Gil. "Maybe we should head back before we get boxed in."

"According to the map, this canyon should open up just

west of here. That's where the pass is coming through."

Against her better judgment, Jessie let Gil lead them on. There was no concrete reason for her unease, yet Ki had felt uneasy, too. While she would sometimes doubt her own feelings, she had found Ki's sixth sense to be always on the mark. Still, turning back at this point would mean the waste of a day; they would have to set out tomorrow and cover the same ground, and every delay, no matter how minor, was another victory for the saboteurs. Jessie, Ki, and Gil would stay on their guard and forge ahead.

Soon the stream opened into a small basin surrounded by towering cliffs. A spring cascaded down the rock walls and together with the stream formed a deep pond in the center. Jessie, Ki, and Gil reined in at the mouth of the basin. The pond itself was of no consequence. Regardless of its depth, they could swim it if necessary. It was the channel feeding out that was the problem. As Gil had predicted, the canyon did open up, but it did so by a series of precarious rapids and waterfalls. From their position it was difficult to gauge the drop. They could see the land leveling off in the distance, but the number of drops and their heights were impossible to tell.

Gil fumbled with his chart, unrolling it in his lap. "Damn! There's no indication of this at all."

"Just the same, here it is," Jessie replied tactfully. "But how could anyone miss it?" she asked incredulously.

"That's about the only thing I can answer," he said as he disgustedly rolled up the map and put it away. "The survey was made along the right of way—from the north. Following the proposed layout of the tracks, this stretch is by-passed. The tracks cross east of here and then down there in the southwest, so the waterfalls were never charted. To the track, it's a gradual dip in elevation."

"I'm afraid it's anything but gradual," Jessie said tersely.

"There's only one way to tell." Gil started his horse forward.

Ki called out quickly. "Wait! The current will force you

right down that chute. If it's too steep a drop, there'll be no way of turning back."

Gil reined in. "You're right. I don't know what got into me. But there seems to be no other way out."

Ki was carefully searching the cliff walls and coming to the same conclusion. Suddenly he caught a glint of light from high atop the canyon ledge. The sun reflecting off a metallic object.

"Get down!" he yelled quickly. He saw the flash, even before he heard the gun's recoil. It was followed by other quick shots. They were easily out of range of the six-guns, and there would have been no immediate danger, if it were not for the horses. The horses, being work animals, were never broken to gunfire, and at the sound of the first shots, they immediately broke.

It took all of Ki's strength and balance to bring his whirling horse under control. Gil was barely managing to hang on to his horse as it reared high in the air. Jessie, however, was faring considerably worse. Unaccustomed to riding untrained horses, she was taken totally by surprise when her brown roan bolted into the water. She was fighting for control when the horse stumbled and slid down a slippery rock. Jessie, already precariously balanced, went flying over the horse's head and into the cold water of the pond.

At the sound of the splash, Ki turned, edged his horse closer to the pond, and then dived from his saddle into the deep waters. The current was carrying Jessie into the center of the basin, and she would soon be in range of the gunmen who were still firing from the top of the canyon. Even more dangerous, it was carrying her down the chute that would send her over the falls. Jessie was a good swimmer, but her efforts were hardly a match for the strong current. Using all her strength, she was able to slow her progress, but after a few moments she'd tire and would speed to the falls as quickly as a fallen twig.

Realizing this, Ki struck out on a course that would intersect Jessie's path before the falls. It was safer to be set and prepared to catch her than to swim after her, try to grab her, and then have to fight the currents back. Ki never took his eyes off Jessie. Swimming swiftly ahead of the current, he kept his head above water, his eyes always trained on his quarry. When Jessie stopped struggling and began to be carried along by the flowing water, he was well positioned. He treaded water and only had to wait a moment for Jessie to come floating into his outstretched arms. He grabbed her quickly and pulled her into him.

"Relax; you're safe now," he said reassuringly, though it wasn't entirely true. He made sure to keep her head above water.

"I'm tired, but okay," Jessie responded between coughs. Her arms were wrapped tightly around his neck.

Together they floated closer to the falls. The shooting had stopped; it no longer seemed necessary. It appeared evident that nature would take care of what the gunmen failed to do. Moving swiftly towards the precipice, Jessie and Ki seemed goners for sure.

Now that the shooting had stopped, Gil regained control of his horse. Jessie and Ki were in a jam and he had to do something. Without hesitation, Gil dug his spurs into his horse and they went flying into the water.

Meanwhile, Ki had managed to wedge one foot against a submerged boulder. It was not a secure hold, but by constantly shifting his weight, he was able to use the force of the water to keep himself pressed against the rock. It was only a matter of time, though, before he would lose his balance and be flung back into the raging current. When he saw Gil approaching, his first reaction was relief, but he quickly realized that Gil could offer little assistance. As Gil moved closer, Ki could just make out the words he was shouting.

"On horseback . . . we'll have a chance . . . gimme your hand."

The horse would absorb much of the impact. If they could hang on, and the drop wasn't too steep—and if the rocks weren't too sharp—they might have a chance. Ki thought he might be able to fight the current, but it would take all his strength, and keeping Jessie's head out of the water would be difficult. "Take Jessie," he yelled to Gil.

"But the current—you'll drown!"

Ki was shaking his head. "You'll have a better chance if it's just you two."

There was no more time for discussion. Gil's horse was just a few feet away. Ki mentally planned the movement; soon there would be no time for thinking. The front grip would be the horse's bit; the last chance, if he missed, would be the horse's tail. With Jessie still clinging to him, Ki pushed off the rock. He hoped he had timed it right. A bit too early and he might get pushed under by the size and momentum of the horse. If too late, he would miss altogether.

The timing seemed perfect, but as Ki reached out, the frantic horse shied away. Ki was unable to grab a firm hold on the horse's slippery mane. He felt Gil reach out and grab Jessie's arm, but unless Ki could check their progress, Gil might not be able to hold on. Ki pivoted quickly and hooked an elbow around Gil's leg. He felt Jessie being lifted off.

"Got her!" Gil announced triumphantly. Ki remained wrapped around Gil's leg. "Are you sure you . . ." Gil started to say.

Ki nodded. "I have some business to take care of." Then, releasing his hold, Ki slid under the water.

Gil lifted Jessie out of the current's grasp and swung her up and into the front of the saddle. It was not the most comfortable position, but Gil reckoned it would be the most secure. Once he had her in place, he turned and watched for Ki, but before he saw him surface, they were at the edge of the first thundering falls. Had there been more time, Gil might have felt fear, but he had just enough time to lean forward and grab the horse around the neck. Their safety was dependent upon staying on the horse, and by locking his arms around the animal's neck he was also pinning Jessie between himself and the horse. He pressed his legs hard against the horse's ribs, and then with a yell they were over the edge.

In the first moments they seemed to be flying over the water. Almost instantly, they were caught amidst the cascading waters, a series of buckets crashing on their heads. The shower ended abruptly with a huge splash that sent both horse and riders well below the surface of the water. Gil had been braced for the impact, but was unprepared for the deep dunking. Just as he was afraid he might lose his hold, the horse broke through to the surface.

Gil released his hold and let out a triumphant hoot. "We made it!" They had survived a sixty-foot drop and Gil was feeling on top of the world. Jessie, still weak, turned and smiled. "The worst is over," Gil said, looking back at the falls. He gave a reassuring squeeze to her shoulders. "We'll be okay."

The river was narrowing and it was Gil's hunch that the next drop would be smaller. His concern was that the pool of water would be shallower. He leaned forward again and wrapped his arms around the horse. "Piece of cake," he whispered to no one in particular.

They went over the edge, but managed to stay out ahead of the falling waters. During the drop, only about twenty-five feet, Jessie kept her eyes open. Without the water falling about her head and blinding her sight, she was able to make a quick assessment of the terrain. There was probably one more fall, but the land was already leveling off, and there were spots along the bank where they would be able to climb.

They hit the water and Jessie felt Gil's grip tighten around her. She marveled at the power of his arms and, for a moment, her mind wandered. She imagined what it would be like to be held by those arms, their bodies locked together. They were only submerged briefly, and as they reached the surface, her thoughts returned to the present. Her eyes searched along the edge of the water and found a large, flat boulder with a gradual slope leading up to the bank.

"Gill, I think we can make it up over there," she said, pointing. But the horse of its own volition was already heading for the rock.

Jessie waited till they were safely up on dry land before she swiveled in the saddle and threw her arms around Gil. As they embraced, Gil began to slip from the horse. He reached out and grabbed for the horn.

"Whoa! I'd hate to make it through all that, only to crack my head open falling from the saddle." They both began to laugh heartily. Gil swung himself down from the saddle and then pulled Jessie down into his arms.

Jessie stared into his warm brown eyes, then leaned forward, and pressed her lips against his. His lips were tender and warm against hers, and a wave of well-being swept over her. She would have liked losing herself in the sensation, but there were still things to attend to. Reluctantly, she pulled away. "What about Ki?" she asked.

"He had something he wanted to do. I'm sure he'll be okay."

He would be okay, Jessie told herself. Still, she wouldn't be able to relax until she knew that for certain.

★

Chapter 6

Ki swam along the bottom of the pond. Darting among the underwater rocks, he was spared some of the water's turbulence. With a continuous, forced exhale he was able to make it practically to the base of the canyon wall. If anyone were looking for him, he would be watching the opposite side, so Ki had no intention of returning to the edge of the pond.

To the untrained eye, the canyon was a sheer slab of rock, unclimbable and unassaultable. But Ki was able to discern tiny cracks all the way up the face of the wall. The three had started out to get the saboteurs. Ki planned on doing just that. He needed only the shallowest of holds for a finger or two or a slight irregularity for his feet. He was positive the rock offered that much.

Ki made slow, steady progress. He would flatten his body against the rock and follow a fissure until he could reach up, grab another hold, and pull himself to a higher level. Sometimes there was no room for more than his fingertips; other times he would wedge his whole fist into a crag to get a firm hold. Often he would have to traverse more horizontally than he climbed vertically. But he was patient and knew that success was within his grasp. It was also very necessary. But right now, he did not dwell on that. It was an arduous climb that required all his concentration. The only thing that concerned Ki was the next crack. He was keenly aware of his center of gravity and the forces working against him. A tiny shift in his weight, no matter how small, would upset his balance and send him to his death.

He had not looked down since he started his climb and in the past ten minutes had not looked up beyond the next hold and then each subsequent one. Therefore, it was with a little surprise that Ki found himself just below the top of the precipice. Ironically, after scaling an almost vertical wall, he now faced the most dangerous part of the climb. Depending upon the position of the gunmen, Ki could be a sitting target as he swung himself up and over the edge.

Ki waited. After the strenuous climb, he rested his tired body and listened for any clue as to the men's whereabouts. The voices he heard could not have been more than ten yards from his position on the edge.

"Relax, Sneed. No one could have survived the falls."

"What about the Chinaman?"

"Hell, I bagged him myself, saw him go under, too," the first man said cockily. Ki suppressed a smile.

"Well, I'm going down to see for myself."

"You'll be lucky if you find the bodies." There was a slight pause and then the man continued with a snicker, "Unless, of course, you're hopin' to find that female." There was sharp laughter.

"Shut up, Perkins. I'm just goin' to make sure the job's done. Tag along if you like." The voice held a bit of nervous tension to it.

"Naw, I don't care for dead meat."

"I told you to keep your dirty mouth shut!" The man was being pushed close to the breaking point.

"All right, Sneed, take it easy," Perkins said quickly. "Didn't mean nothin' by it."

"I'm gonna have a look, and if the girl's still alive, I'm gonna have myself a good time. Now, you comin' or not?" Ki could hear the man climb into his saddle.

"I told you I don't care for dead—" Perkins caught himself quickly. "They're dead, Sneed. I'll just sit here."

Ki heard the horse gallop away. It was both good and bad. He now had to deal with only one adversary in that vulnerable moment when he would climb into view. But he would also have to pursue Sneed and overtake him before he got to Jessie—if, of course, she were still alive. He had to deal with his opponent quickly. That in itself posed no problem, but it annoyed Ki that again the chance to gain information from a captive would probably be out of the question.

There was no use in waiting longer. Though he would have liked to have rested his exhausted body a bit more, the more he delayed the harder it would be to overtake Sneed. Ki ran through the many possibilities in his head. Once over the top, he would have little time to think. The better prepared he was, the easier the task could be accomplished. What if Perkins were sitting with his back to him? What if he were standing and facing him?

When he had played out all the scenarios, Ki was ready. He pulled himself up and over the top and silently rolled to his feet. What he was not prepared for was coming face to face with the hulking figure that stood before him.

Perkins, apparently walking to the edge to reaffirm his belief that no one could have survived, was as startled as Ki. He reached for his gun and had it out quickly, but Ki was faster.

Ki dropped to his side, and scissored Perkins' ankles between his legs. Perkins was well over six feet and built like a bull, but it took only a swift movement to topple the weighty hulk. The surprised Perkins threw out his arms to cushion his fall and the gun went flying.

As he tried to sit up, Ki kicked his top leg straight into Perkins' chest. The powerful kick seemed to have little effect; the man was built solidly. Ki was now at a distinct disadvantage. The sheer bulk of his opponent was keeping his bottom leg pinned to the ground. Though his movement was restricted, Ki lashed out with his free leg, delivering rapid kicks to the torso. They connected with mighty snaps, but they didn't have the force of his whole body behind them, and they seemed to be having little effect.

To make matters worse, Perkins' reach exceeded that of Ki's by a good six inches. Perkins stretched his massive arm and grabbed Ki's face. Meaty fingers dug into Ki's eyes. The other hand reached for Ki's throat. Quickly, Ki dug his chin into his chest. That saved him from a stranglehold, but the crushing grip around his face and jaw threatened to crack his skull open like a shattered walnut. Perkins continued to apply the viselike pressure and, as he did so, drew Ki closer to him. That was his mistake.

Ki brought his left hand up and over the fleshy paw that covered his face. He sought out and found a pressure point between the delicate bones of the hand. He dug his thumb in hard and twisted back. There was a quiet groan of pain, and the hand peeled off his face. At the same moment, Ki swung his other elbow up into Perkins' jaw. There was a resounding crack and Perkins rolled over in pain.

Ki scrambled to his feet, and Perkins, despite his great size, was standing just as quickly. Like an enraged bull, he lowered his head and came charging at Ki. That was his final mistake. By virtue of his extreme bulk, a man that size is used to simply overpowering his rival. But Ki had no intention of opposing the force that came headlong at him. He would take Perkins' might and turn it against him.

As the pair of large arms began to close around Ki, he grabbed Perkins' shirt, dropped to the ground, and flipped the raging bull into the air. His own momentum carried the dumbfounded Perkins right up to the edge of the cliff. He shook his head, trying to clear it, and rose slowly to his feet. In the end it was the man's massive size that led to his downfall. The loose clay underneath Perkins began to crumble, and in the next instant, as he began to take a step, the whole edge gave way. Perkins tumbled backward and vanished from sight.

Without further delay, Ki hopped on Perkins' horse and hightailed it after Sneed.

"The first thing we should do is try to dry these clothes," Gil said, holding his wet shirt away from his body.

"I'll start gathering some wood," Jessie offered.

"The fire'll be waiting for you," Gil promised.

When Jessie returned, Gil, true to his word, had made a little clearing and there was a small fire going. Jessie dropped her armload of branches and sat down next to Gil.

"It doesn't look like much, but you'll feel warm in no time." Gil already had his boots and socks laid out by the fire.

"A good cup of coffee wouldn't hurt."

Gil laughed. "I haven't had a good cup of coffee in months."

"Well, I'd settle for a hot one."

"I don't want to leave you here by yourself, or else I'd go and try to get our horses."

"I'm fine, Gil, really. It's just nice to think about warm coffee," Jessie said with an apologetic smile.

"And a biscuit," Gil added wistfully.

"But right now this is beginning to feel awfully nice." Jessie reached out and threw a handful of large twigs into the fire. They caught quickly, the small yellow flames dancing briefly and then dying down into deep red embers. At regular intervals Jessie and Gil piled wood on the fire.

Slowly the warmth melted away the shock. They both sat in silence, grateful to be alive after coming so close to death. Was it luck? Jessie stared into the flames. Was there, as Ki believed, a set time and place, and this simply was not hers. She had come close to death often, but it seemed quite real now. Maybe that was because this was the present, and the other encounters were dwelling in her memory. She looked at Gil. Did he have anything to do with her feelings? She caught him staring at her. Did he feel it too? she wondered.

They stared at each other silently and then Gil started to speak. His voice was faint and he stopped. Instead, he got up and cleared his throat. "I'm going to go look for some bigger logs. We're going through this stuff pretty fast."

Jessie couldn't break the spell she seemed to be under, so she said nothing and watched him walk away. There was a soft breeze, and the slight chill made her very aware of her body—the wet jeans that clung to her thighs, the plain cotton blouse that was drying against the round softness of her breasts. She removed her shirt and held it over the fire. It would be dry soon. As she stood close to the flames, the warmth felt good against her bare skin. Above the crackling of the wood, she thought she heard something and brought her shirt in front of her chest.

"Gil?" There was no answer. She looked around and then heard it again, a distinctive crack of a twig. "Ki?" Suddenly, Sneed emerged from the bushes.

"Well, what have we here?" Sneed said. He had his gun pointed right at her.

"Drop the shirt," Sneed said with a leer. Jessie looked around furtively. Sneed caught the gesture and let out a vicious laugh. "Don't be waitin' for your gentleman friend to help. I took care of him."

Something went limp inside her. She lowered her shirt that was covering her naked chest.

"Oh, my," Sneed said in admiration. He took a step forward and smiled. His teeth were stained and dirty.

Suddenly, Jessie's resolve returned. This was not her time. As long as the cartel existed and continued plying their evil, she would be there fighting it. That, she was certain, was her destiny. The filthy beast who approached her was not a man, but a cartel lizard that needed stamping out. Then a thought came to her; the man had no knife and she had not heard a gunshot. That meant Gil was probably only knocked out. The realization gave her added strength.

Sneed must have seen something in her eyes. "Don't try anything," he said icily. "I'd just as soon pump you full of lead first and then drill you with my rod." He stood up close to her and ran the cold metal barrel of his revolver around her pink nipples. "Perk'll be sorry he missed this." His breath was becoming short and rapid. "Now, drop them jeans."

Jessie began to wiggle out of her tight pants. Sneed, already excited, began to unbutton the fly of his own jeans. But it was not a job that could be easily accomplished with one hand. He brought his other hand down to his crotch. The instant his gun was lowered, Jessie struck, poking her two fingers deep into Sneed's eyes.

"You bitch!" he yelled loudly.

Jessie slammed her foot into his groin. It was not a powerful kick, but it was placed well. Sneed doubled over and bellowed in pain, but still held his gun.

Jessie quickly reached into the fire and pulled out a burning branch. As soon as Sneed pulled his hand away from his face, she shoved the glowing poker right back at his eyes. There was the searing sound of burning flesh.

Sneed let loose with a scream. "I'll kill you! I'll kill you, you bitch!" He was whirling in circles, shrieking. Blindly, he pointed the gun and began shooting.

Jessie ducked and, as he turned, shoved the glowing stick against his hand. Another yell of pain—the gun dropped. Jessie snatched it up quickly and took a few steps back. Through the blur of pain and burned flesh, Sneed must have seen her image because he was now rushing directly at her, still screaming "I'll kill you, you bitch, rip you apart—"

She leveled the gun and pulled the trigger. *Click!* The gun went off harmlessly, the hammer falling on an empty cylinder. Jessie took another step back, but now Sneed was strangely quiet. She backed up again and Sneed toppled, face first, into the dirt at her feet. A shiny silver *shuriken* lay embedded halfway into the base of his skull.

She looked up and went running to Ki. As he slid off his horse, Jessie went rushing into his arms. Relief poured through her. She was saved; Ki was alive.

"Ki," she said.

He held her by the shoulders and gently pushed her back in order to see that she was unharmed. He didn't seem to notice she was only half dressed.

"I'm okay, Ki," she said to reassure him.

"And Gil?"

"I think he's okay, too. I'll get my shirt and we'll look for him."

Without too much trouble they found him, slumped under a tree. The pile of wood he had collected was scattered in the dirt around him. Ki lifted him over his shoulder and carried him down to the stream.

The cold water quickly revived him. Dazed, Gil looked from Jessie to Ki. "What happened?" he asked shakily.

"You were probably hit from behind," Jessie informed him. "One of the cartel's men." Gil was rubbing the back of his neck. "Here, keep this against it." She handed him a wet rag, formerly the lower half of her sleeve.

"Do you think you can stand?" Ki asked.

Gil nodded and then winced with pain. "Easy," Ki said as he helped him up. "Dizzy?"

This time Gil kept his head still. "No."

"Good. Can you see clearly?"

"Yes."

Ki looked relieved. "You'll have a nasty bump on your head. Other than that, you'll be fine."

Jessie reached out a hand to help steady Gil. "You might have a concussion," she explained.

"There's an advantage to being hardheaded," Gil said in a feeble attempt at humor, though he didn't feel much like laughing.

"Let's get back to the fire, and then we'll see about

getting some food into us," Ki said as he put Gil's arm around his shoulder.

Once back at the fire, Ki left the two and then returned a moment later, leading the two thugs' horses. He unstrapped the bedrolls and brought them to Jessie. "These should make things more comfortable," he said, handing them to her, and then went to search the saddlebags. He found a flask of whiskey and a few pieces of jerky.

He went to Gil and held the flask up to his lips. "Take a sip. It'll do you good." He poured a small amount into Gil's mouth and passed the container to Jessie. "You're looking a bit pale, too."

Jessie took a healthy swig. The whiskey felt warm going down. "Thanks. It feels good."

"This will hold you till dinner." Ki handed her the dried beef. "I'll be back soon." He got up and went to Sneed's body. He picked up the revolver and reloaded it with shells from Sneed's belt. He shoved the gun into his waistband and then dragged Sneed's body into the woods.

Ten minutes later, Jessie heard two shots. Shortly after, Ki stepped out from the underbrush carrying two rabbits and a handful of plants.

"I hope you're hungry," he said with a smile as he held up the two dead animals by their ears.

In no time at all, the rabbits were skinned and roasting on a spit. The aroma of the grilling meat increased their raging appetites. When the rabbits were cooked to perfection, Ki served them with delicate blue flowers and small green leaves that were picked off the bushes he carried back.

"This is terrific," Gil mumbled with a full mouth. "Best rabbit I've had in a long time. And these sure are tasty morsels." He held up one of the blue flowers. "Even the leaves are good," he added after he swallowed.

"Bluebells. Most people don't know they're not only edible, but good for them, too."

"For a meal like this, I'd go through it all again—well, almost," Jessie said with a smile.

Gil tossed a small bone into the fire and stretched out to relax. "I'm feeling mighty content right now."

"Then it's time for dessert," Ki exclaimed. He passed around a handful of bright red berries. "Sorry there aren't more, but the birds beat us." Ki pulled himself onto his feet. "I better get going." Gil turned to him questioningly. "Someone has to get our horses and equipment," Ki explained.

"I'll go with you." Gil started to get up.

"No, you should take it easy. And I want to take the body back. His face is pretty burned, but maybe someone will recognize him."

"I guess you gotta follow every lead."

Ki nodded. He walked into the woods, lifted Sneed's body, walked back, and threw it over the back of the horse. He used a small length of cord to tie his hands and feet under the belly of the animal. Ki made sure the body was secure and then mounted the other horse. "I'll be back by tomorrow evening, so don't let me hold you up."

Gil looked to Jessie, thought a moment, and then turned back to Ki. "We'll be up in Jackass Pass; by evening we'll be at a surveyor's shack in a meadow just west of Fremont Lake."

"Meet you there." Ki swung his horse around and headed out.

★

Chapter 7

The sun was just setting. The color of the sky went from azure blue overhead to a crimson at the horizon. A gentle breeze began to blow. It held the promise of a quite cool evening. After dinner, Jessie and Gil had gone out and collected enough wood to keep the fire blazing through most of the night. Gil threw another log on the fire and watched as the flames licked at and eventually engulfed the fresh wood.

He continued to stare at the fire as he spoke. "Every time we're alone I forget about the rest of the world," he said softly. Jessie sat right beside him, there was no need for anything more than whispers.

"I'd like to feel the same, Gil." There seemed to be genuine regret in her voice.

"But?"

"But there's too much at stake," she answered flatly.

"Can I help?"

"Just finish the railroad," she said with a slight shrug.

"And beyond that?" Gil placed his hands on her shoulders. "I want to help you, Jessie. What is it you're fighting?"

"It's a long story, Gil."

"We have all night; there's plenty of wood."

"Wouldn't you rather just kiss me?" There was a playful tone in her voice, but it was still a serious request.

Gil burst out into a hearty laugh. "Yes, I'd like to kiss you and I'd hate to disappoint you, but right now, I think I want to know what's going on."

"I don't often ask to be kissed, Gil Johnson."

Gil couldn't be sure whether she was teasing him or whether he had seriously offended her. He thought back on his last indiscretion and the time he spent riding alone in the icy water. Still, he sincerely wanted to know about Jessie's problems. He held firm and said nothing.

"And I've never been turned down before," Jessie continued, but now she was smiling sweetly. She appreciated Gil's caring enough to want to talk first. She leaned over and kissed him lightly on the lips. It would be worth the wait, she decided. After they finished talking, she would feel even closer to him, and everything would be even better.

She started her tale at the beginning—with her father Alex and the empire he established with his import/export business. It was while conducting trade in the Orient that Alex first came upon the cartel. Then, as the Starbuck empire grew, the conflict between the Prussian-backed organization and her father intensified. Alex soon realized that the cartel was striving to become entrenched in American politics and business; they already had men of influence in Washington and local governments, and they had lots of international money to buy whatever they needed: men, companies, or legislation. Starbuck enterprises, though, was not without its own power and influence. For a while there seemed to be a stalemate. And that's when the battle turned to the more covert, illegal areas. When Jessie was just a little girl, her mother was killed by the cartel. Her death was avenged, and the battle became a full-scale war that eventually led to the death of her father.

"And you've been carrying on the fight ever since?" Gil said, absorbed by the drama.

Jessie nodded. "Me and Ki."

"How does Ki fit in?"

Jessie smiled as she reminisced. "My father brought him over from Japan years ago to be my bodyguard. He turned out to be a good teacher and a close friend."

"A very devoted one, it seems." There was no trace of jealousy in Gil's words.

Jessie continued, "Sometimes I think that Ki is the son my father never had, and maybe the Circle Star is the home that Ki never had. I like to think that the ranch is as much a home to him as it is to me."

"And there's no one else to help you fight the cartel?" Gil inquired incisively.

Jessie, at first, thought to evade the question. She had a good hunch what Gil was really asking. "The nature of the cartel is such that we can't accuse them openly. We have to fight them on their own terms." As Jessie finished, she realized that there was no reason to hide anything from Gil. "There's also a federal lawman in Colorado"—she hesitated briefly—"Marshal Longarm, who is a friend of the family and who knows of the cartel and helps whenever possible. But for the most part Ki and I stop the cartel by ourselves."

Gil thought for a moment. "I reckon you do get around a lot. It sounds like the cartel is trying to get their hands in everything."

Jessie nodded. "We have to stay on our toes. We never know where the cartel is going to try to get another foothold." She thought for a moment of all the various places and the different tactics used by the cartel to further their evil plan and acquire more power here in America. "They've tried grabbing grazing land in Wyoming, silver mines in Colorado, control of the docks of San Francisco, and they've hired outlaws, rustlers, and bandits in just about all the states and territories."

"That's an awful big burden, Jessie," Gil said sympathetically. "Ki seems suited for this, but you, you're..." He hesitated, searching for the right word.

"You don't think I'm as tough as Ki?"

"I hope not." That put a smile on Jessie's face. "I think of you as being more ladylike, more feminine," Gil added.

"I'm all feminine, Gil." Her tongue moistened her dry lips; her voice was low and purring. "And right now I'm not feeling very tough at all."

Gil leaned over to her. Jessie closed her eyes and then felt Gil's lips on hers—their tongues meeting, caressing, dancing. When Gil's lips released their hold on hers, Jessie inhaled deeply. During the embrace her breath seemed to have been sucked away.

"Ever since I first saw you, I've wanted to do that, Jessie."

"I know."

"Am I that transparent?" Gil wondered out loud.

"No, I felt the same, sweetheart."

The tenderness in her voice made Gil sweep her back into his arms. The embrace was even more passionate; they pressed close as their hands explored each other's contours. Jessie's breasts were swelling with desire, her nipples growing taut under her blouse. She yearned to press her bare skin against Gil, to feel the warmth of his body. Her hands moved to the buttons of his shirt and she was soon running her hands across his strong, hairy chest. Jessie lowered her head and began planting soft, tender kisses across his chest, her lips barely brushing his skin. The feel of his hairs against her lips increased her desire. She flicked her tongue across Gil's tiny, firm nipples. He let out a groan and pulled away from her. "Don't," she started to say.

"I want to throw more wood on the fire. Another minute of that and I wouldn't have been able to get up."

Night had fallen softly and the dark cloudless sky was ablaze with twinkling stars. The fire had died down to a mound of glowing embers. Gil stood up and piled a heap of wood on the fire. "It's going to be a long, enjoyable night and I don't think I'll be able to tear myself away from you later."

Jessie ran her hand up his thigh and felt a tremor of anticipation rush through her as her hand brushed over his crotch. Even through his pants she could feel his growing manhood, hard as an iron spike. She could feel her own readiness between her legs. Uncontrollably, she squeezed Gil's shaft.

He moaned softly. She began to undo the buttons of his pants. The fresh wood caught fire just as she freed Gil's shaft from the confines of his jeans. It was thick and powerful, and in the firelight, its head glowed a deep red. She moved to encircle it with her mouth, but Gil was already stepping back to remove his clothes.

Gil hopped on one leg as he struggled to pull off his boots, and Jessie let out a giggle. "I'm sorry, Gil, but you look so funny hopping around like that." He turned to her and she caught her breath. "But there's nothing funny about your body. It's very handsome and very manly."

Gil was at rigid attention and Jessie could almost see it throb as he moved over her. "I'm sorry this is all we have," he said as he spread out the bedrolls next to the fire. "You deserve a large, lush bed with clean sheets and big, soft pillows."

"You're everything I need, Gil." She lay back and began undoing her blouse.

Gil kneeled over her. "I'll do that, Jessie." He began to undress her, admiring her beauty as he went along. Her face soft and smooth, with its high cheekbones and perfect smile, was a cameo of beauty. Her hair, now a lustrous golden, swirled down onto her ivory shoulders. As her shirt was opened and pushed back, her budding nipples felt the coolness of the night air, but that was soon replaced by the warmth of Gil's mouth. He sucked hungrily at her breasts as his hand undid her tight jeans and pushed them downward. Gil went from one nipple to the other and then let his tongue travel down her flat stomach to the wisps of soft down that poked above her pants.

With Gil's help Jessie shimmied out of her jeans. It was now Gil's turn to gasp in admiration. "You're so beautiful, so perfect." His eyes devoured every inch of her. "And your eyes are so gorgeous."

Jessie felt the weight of his body as he lowered himself onto her. His lips pressed against hers and she was once again lost in his embrace, but she let out a loud gasp as she felt his hardness press against her mound and then penetrate. Her eyes opened wide; she felt so unbelievably filled. Her hands roamed over Gil's body. The strong thighs she had fantasized about earlier were now moving hard against her own legs. Her nails traced patterns up and down their length. She could hear the sound their bodies made as their thighs slapped together, but she had no sense of it; her feelings were focused deep inside her. Every movement, every thrust, seemed to satisfy even more than the previous one. Jessie's body was moving in perfect harmony with Gil's. She arched her back, rocked her hips, and matched every powerful thrust. Gil began pumping into her with the persistance of a spike driver, each stroke boring deep. Jessie would shiver as he filled her and then catch her breath momentarily before he would drive his solid pole right back to the hilt.

The blazing fire could not match the heat the two lovers were feeling. The world began to blur as Jessie became consumed in a wave of growing pleasure. She closed her eyes and felt herself drift along. It wasn't long before she knew she was at that point of no return, the point where the wave would overtake her and come crashing down on her. She grabbed hold of his ass and pressed him tight into her. She wanted to feel him deep, deep...And the wave broke and washed away, leaving every muscle, every cell, bathed in the aftermath of total release.

Stars were everywhere. She opened her eyes and only saw their shimmer and then her eyes focused and she saw Gil, his smile alive with its own sparkle. She could still feel him rocking on top of her.

"I distinctly remember Ki telling you to take it easy." Her voice was thick and husky. "You shouldn't be exerting yourself like this."

"Chopping wood is an exertion. This is an honor . . . and a pleasure."

Jessie lifted her head and gave him a quick kiss. Even now, when she felt so utterly blissful, Gil's charm still put a new smile on her face. "Still, I want you to take it easy." With that, she rolled him over on his back. Gil was a willing accomplice and Jessie was able to sit astride his powerful legs without having him slip from within her.

"Now, I want you to relax," she said soothingly, but her actions were designed for everything but. Supporting her weight on her knees, she began to rotate slowly about Gil's meaty pivot. Gil reached up for her firm breasts and massaged them tenderly, but he soon put an arm around her and lowered her warm, ripe nipple into his waiting mouth.

Gil's passion began to increase. He took hold of her hips and held her fast while he drove into her. Jessie realized that he was soon going to reach his peak and probably take her along with him.

"Relax . . ." She sat up and then leaned back, further impaling herself on his hot spear. "Just lie there." Then Jessie began to do what few women can—a technique prized by many, but mastered by very few.

Gil began to protest, but was quickly silenced. His shaft was being squeezed by Jessie's inner muscles. He was held in a firm grip. The warmth of her body would methodically grasp and release him. "Oooh," he sighed softly.

Inside her, Jessie could feel him swell. She reached behind her and held Gil's bulging sack. He let out another moan. Each twitch of his manhood deep inside her excited her almost beyond control, but she remained perfectly still, except for those inner muscles, sucking, squeezing, milking the essence of him. And when she felt they could both stand it no longer, her fingers closed around his warm pouch.

She felt a sudden spurt and then was aware only of her

own tremors, wracking her body with sensual delight. After her initial spasm passed, she could still feel Gil gushing within her, and another reverberation swept through her.

Jessie collapsed onto Gil. "Gil, for now nothing else exists."

Gil wrapped his arms around her and drew up the bedroll. They slept that way until morning.

When Ki made it back to the railhead, the moon was high in the sky. He headed directly toward the camp. The horses could be fetched tomorrow. Now there were more urgent matters. During the ride Ki had wondered whether the run-in with the cartel toughs was a coincidence. It might have been just an accident that they were spotted by Perkins, or it could have been a cleverly planned ambush. The trail had been easy to follow up until the stream, at which point the search might have gone either way. But if the gunmen had known which direction Gil intended to head, an ambush could have been planned.

But whether the trap had been planned or lucky, the toughs were privy to some inside information. As Gil had mentioned, they knew the lay of the land and, more important, they knew to set fire to Ki's tent. That they did it the very first night indicated to Ki that someone within the camp and probably in the know was giving the orders. It was quite possible that if the attack had been planned someone would be up and waiting for some word.

It was a long shot, but it was the only thing Ki had to go on. He hunkered down in the timbers that overlooked the camp. He placed himself in a position that afforded a view of the whole camp, but was deep enough into the woods so that he would not be spotted. He leaned against the back of a tree and waited.

He kept himself alert by running questions through his head. Was the cartel really involved? Who was the cartel spy? What were they hoping to gain? Where would they strike next? Though he approached each question from different angles, he still could not come up with any solid answers. But he had hunches.

When he exhausted the possibilities Ki shifted his mind to Gil's caboose and of the warm bed that would be waiting for him there. A false dawn was beginning to break; Ki could still catch an hour of sleep. He thought of Cynthia lying there, her soft chest rising and falling with each breath. He could feel her warmth next to him. He smiled, remembering that night and thinking of future nights. But then he thought of the fire in his tent, of the saboteurs, and of the cartel. There was still much to do. He would go down and fix himself a hearty breakfast. There would be time for Cynthia later. It was a promise he made to himself and intended to keep.

He headed straight for the mess tent. Pops was already awake and firing up the stove. "Morning, Pops," Ki said as he dismounted. "Coffee hot yet?"

"Just about. Looks like you could do with some, too," Pops said as he gave him the once-over. He shifted his gaze to the body tied across the horse. "Don't reckon it'll help your friend there any."

"That's one of the men who set fire to my tent."

"And the others?" Pops asked with a raise of an eyebrow.

"Over a cliff."

Pops nodded understandingly. "Well, come on in and we'll rustle you up something more than coffee."

"Pops, you don't recognize him do you?"

The cook circled around the dead man and bent over to peer into his face. Pops stood up and shook his head. "Can't say I do. And I got a mind for faces. Why, once there was this Irish grader, a big hulk of a man, but then they were all big men, but he had a mark right here." Pops pointed to his cheek and then proceeded to spin another yarn about the old days. Ki listened politely while he ate, but after he had consumed his fill, he thanked the cook and took his leave.

It was not a promising sign for the cook not to recognize

the dead man. But Ki took hold of the corpse-laden horse and headed for Spike's tent to check with him.

Spike was just stepping out of his tent as Ki approached. He studied the body and then indifferently pulled his suspenders up over his shoulders. It was impossible to read any reaction on the foreman's face.

"Recognize him?" Ki asked.

Spike shook his head and began to walk toward the mess tent. Ki followed him. "It's one of the saboteurs." There was no response from Spike. "You don't seem very concerned," Ki pressed, trying to get some kind of sign out of him.

"Well, then, he got what he deserved," Spike stated flatly.

"But there are a lot of men getting what they don't deserve."

Spike turned quickly. The scowl on his face put Ki on instant alert. It was a look he had seen many times in saloons, bunkhouses, and on the range. It was a look that often left a man lying face down in the dirt.

But Spike's anger released itself with a bitter laugh. "I've been working the roads for twenty-three years, and I deserve more than a hard cot and a handful of calluses."

"There are innocent men becoming the victims of sabotage," Ki exclaimed.

The anger was returning to Spike. "We're all innocent victims, friend, even the dumb coolies. The bosses get rich, and we break our backs for a cheap bottle of whiskey."

"Men are dying needlessly. Don't you want to stop it?"

"I'll stop it in my own way!"

Was that an open admission of some guilt, Ki wondered, or was he trying to read too much into the remark.

"So far you've been nothing but trouble. You've done your share of killin' and it don't seem you're any closer to stoppin' nothin'!" Spike spat into the ground.

"You're wrong about that." Ki's words had just the slightest trace of a threat to them. In truth, Spike was absolutely correct in his assumption that Ki had learned little that would help him stop the sabotage and break the cartel, but Ki felt he held a good enough hand to play the bluff.

Spike spoke with the assurance of a man who was not making idle boasts. "You cross me and you'll be sorry." The burly foreman stood ready for Ki's reply, either in actions or words. None was forthcoming, so he turned and stomped off.

Ki had learned little from their exchange, but his suspicions were fueled. Was Spike so sure of himself that he could almost admit some role in the sabotage, or was he just a bitter disgruntled worker who, having toiled for years, had little to show for it? The cartel thrived on men like that, men who could easily be corrupted. Was Spike already in the cartel's pocket? Was he the man in charge? Had he been approached by a cartel man and was he still sitting on a fence, undecided? Spike rated close scrutiny.

The mess tent was filling up with hungry workers. Ki went inside to say a quick good-bye to Pops. He caught a few looks from the men and could hear the word being spread about the latest incident with the Pinkerton. Ki smiled to himself; he was rustling the bushes and the snake could strike at any moment.

"Pops, could you see to it that someone buries the body. I'm heading back out to meet Gil and Jessie."

The cook nodded. "There's a gunny sack of grub I tied to your saddle. Figured you might be needin' it," he said with a warm smile.

Ki leaned close to Pops and lowered his voice. "Keep an eye on Spike for me, will you?"

Pops stared at the foreman suspiciously and then turned back to Ki. The old cook's eyes twinkled with delight.

★

Chapter 8

"We've had some pretty heavy rains in the last few weeks," Gil explained to Jessie, "and I want to check the erosion along the embankment."

Along with one horse they had managed to locate, Jessie and Gil were walking along a dry gulch that paralleled the path the tracks would follow. Jessie could well imagine a flood turning the cracked, rocky river bed into a torrent of rushing waters.

Periodically Gil would stop and make a notation in a small notebook.

"You don't need to take a compass reading?" Jessie asked eventually.

Gil smiled modestly. "I have my own markings. I've been through here so many times, I know the right of way like a hungry nag knows her way to the barn."

"And yesterday?" Jessie couldn't resist the playful tease.

"You mean surprise waterfalls?" he asked and Jessie nodded. "Not along the right of way," Gil stated casually.

"Of course."

They walked along in a contented silence. The closeness they shared during the night continued to grow as they spent the day working together.

"This is really the unsung part of the job," Gil explained as he slid the notebook back into his vest pocket. "The actual laying of the tracks gets all the attention, but to me it's a little too mechanical. Problems come up, but they're not new ones, and you're always close to a solution." He swept his gaze across the virgin land that surrounded them. "No, to me this is the heart of it all."

Standing in this mostly uncharted terrain, Jessie knew exactly what he meant.

Gil continued. "You're out in wild, untouched land, and then suddenly you see a path around a mountain or over a ridge, and you start playing with it. You blast here, you put a trestle there, and soon you can start seeing the tracks, real as life. They stretch out, far as the eye can see. That's the magic of it..." His voice trailed off. "I guess I'm just a dreamer at heart," he added boyishly.

"We're all dreamers, Gil. All of us who see something that can be but isn't, or who think we can build a better way. The West was settled by dreamers. The world was conquered by dreamers."

Gil's face lit up. "Thanks, Jessie. I reckon I don't feel so childish now."

"Be proud of it, Gil."

"My job also has its practical side. The locating plays a crucial part in the eventual success of the railroad."

"I thought all railroads laid their tracks based on the fact that the shortest distance between two points is a straight line."

Gil broke into a broad smile. "Many of them did, and many of 'em went bankrupt. The construction costs of a railroad are only the beginning. More often than not, the operating expenses make or break a line."

"Well, that seems right enough, but—"

"But they never considered that when surveying a route,"

Gil interrupted excitedly. "They'd go with the most direct line and wind up with too steep a grade to operate efficiently. Nowadays many of us choose to lay a few extra miles of track and keep the grade gradual."

Jessie thought of the train ride up. "That explains all the trestles and switchbacks coming up here."

"Right! It's not just theory. It wouldn't surprise me a bit if the Oregon Central goes bust before the year is out."

"The Oregon Central?" Jessie inquired.

"The only other railroad in these parts that goes out to the Pacific. They'd be sitting pretty except for the grade. Their engines can't haul enough freight to make it pay."

"Why can't they rebuild?"

"If they could raise enough money they would, but the stockholders rarely go for that. No one wants to throw good money after bad. And by then we'll be up and running. There'll be no need for an Oregon Central."

A slow realization began to dawn on Jessie. "Gil, do you know who owns the Oregon Central?"

"Some firm in the East, I think."

"Not an individual?"

Gil shook his head. "No, I think it's a shipping company. I seem to recall some cracks about steamships on rails—"

"It all makes sense now!" Jessie was exhuberant.

"What does?"

"See, Gil, I thought the cartel was sabotaging the Wood River to stop the shipment of Starbuck lumber. But that never made much sense; there were better, more direct methods."

"Like destroying the mills," suggested Gil.

"Exactly. But now I realize that was just the gravy on the plate. They're after the meat and potatoes."

"The Wood River!"

Jessie nodded. "What happens if the sabotage continues?"

"We run out of money, or men willing to work, or both. It means the end of the Wood River."

"And what happens to the land grants awarded to Commodore Whiting and the railroad."

"They get auctioned off or reassigned."

They practically said it together: "To the Oregon Central!"

Their jubilation passed quickly. "But Jessie, even if we know what's behind it, we're still at the mercy of the saboteurs."

"True, but it's a start. We'll have to stay one step ahead all the time."

"If the cartel is half as bad as you say, we better stop them as soon as possible."

"Believe me, Gil, they'll stop at nothing to get what they want."

"My work is just about finished here. Why don't we mount up and head back? Ki should be getting there soon, too."

Jessie swung atop the horse, then dropped her feet from the stirrups, and inched forward against the pommel. There was just enough room for Gil to squeeze in behind her. Once in the saddle, he slipped his feet into the stirrups and reached his arms around Jessie to take hold of the reins.

"Comfortable?" Gil asked.

"I've never had a better fitting saddle."

As they rode through the pass, Jessie began to look at things as a railroad locator would. There would be a trestle here, she thought, and maybe another there. Or would they blast through that mountain? As they came up and over a ridge, she could easily visualize the long, narrow trail of rails stretching out across the plateau. Off in the distance, she could see a thin wisp of white smoke. As the approaching train grew nearer, she could begin to hear the *clackety-clack* of the wheels and then the churning of the steam engine as it pulled its string of cars tirelessly westward. Coach cars, baggage cars, freight cars. People with dreams of starting new lives. Families and loners, homesteaders, ranchers, tradesmen, skilled and unskilled workers, all honest, hard-working people. And, of course, there were those looking to live off others. In short, civilization, with its mixed blessings, was coming to this beautiful land once considered a wasteland by many. And it came on the railroad.

Her perspective shifted and she viewed the approaching train as the plains Indians must once have viewed the great iron horse that invaded their homeland. But she knew she couldn't blame the railroads. You couldn't stop progress. Years before, settlers had come in covered wagons; others had sailed around the Horn. Where there was a will, there was a way. How long ago was it when anything west of the Mississippi was a vast uncharted unknown? It wasn't all that long ago, Jessie realized, that the gentle grasslands of Kentucky were considered the frontier. Men like Daniel Boone were pioneers of that West, a land that Jessie couldn't help but think of as tame and sedate by comparison. It was an unknown and strange world that the Europeans came to settle. And now people were coming to settle here.

She envisioned the crowded streets of Philadelphia here among the mountains. The trees felled, the waters dammed, the mountains blocked from view by rows of factories. She had to laugh at herself for getting so carried away. But as an eagle drifted high on a wind current, she wondered what really would happen. She couldn't help feeling a small tinge of sadness.

"It's almost a shame," she said softly.

"What is?"

"What the railroad might do to this land."

"Sometimes I feel that, too, but this is man's destiny. But I wouldn't worry too much, Jessie, for there aren't enough people to fill up all the beautiful spots out here."

"I guess you're right, Gil."

The afternoon air was quiet and still. High above, white, billowy clouds seemed to hang motionless against the pale blue sky. Jessie let the warm rays of the sun softly beat her conjectures out of her mind, and the steady swaying of the horse lulled her into a tranquil state. She closed her eyes and drifted.

A moment or a mile later, Jessie was unsure which, she became equally aware of two very pleasant sensations. The first was a warmth that was slowly spreading through her and very clearly originated between her legs. The second was the stiff rod that was pressing firmly into her lower back. Each movement of the horse brought her pleasure. Either she moved forward against the warm, leather pommel or her back would push against Gil's rigid tool. One movement would excite her mind and the other her physical passion. Her jeans seemed interminably tight. She let out a soft moan.

"I thought you were asleep," Gil said softly.

Jessie could feel Gil's sexy voice resonate against her body. "Dreaming, but not asleep," she answered as her hands went to the buttons of her blouse. Her breasts basked in the warmth of the sun; her nipples grew taut as the gentlest of breezes flitted across them. But they did not stay exposed for long; Gil's large well-proportioned hands soon cupped Jessie's soft globes.

"Gil . . ." Jessie began imploringly and then hushed. She couldn't decide if she wanted to stop and get down or continue riding along in ecstasy. In the saddle she was experiencing a deep but level excitement that could—would—continue indefinitely as she hovered close to the edge. If they were to stop, she would be brought to the brink almost instantly . . .

"What, darlin'?"

"It feels so good, but—"

"I'll stop if you'd like." Gil was almost apologetic as he dropped his hands.

"Oh, no," she said quickly, realizing how Gil had misunderstood her hesitation. "I don't want you to stop doing anything. I was thinking that maybe we should stop and stretch out . . . Don't you want to feel good, too, Gil?"

"Don't worry about me."

She reached behind her and felt his throbbing bulge. "I wasn't worried," she said devilishly.

"We're almost there."

Jessie now opened her eyes. They were just entering a large meadow dotted with late-blooming wildflowers.

"There's a small shack just past the opening of this field," continued Gil. "Ki might already be there waiting."

The large patches of bright reds, yellows, and pinks settled it for Jessie. A girl could be swayed by a small bouquet of cut flowers; here was an entire carpet of brilliant colors. "Ki won't mind waiting," she answered. She saw deep purples, made even more splendid by the simple white blossoms that grew alongside.

Jessie wasted no more words and began to stroke Gil's shaft. Gil reined in and slipped down from the horse. Jessie swung around and was sitting sidesaddle. Gil undid her pants and began to slip them off her, showering her legs with kisses as he went. He removed one of her boots. He let her pants dangle from her shod leg. She parted her legs as Gil began to lick his way slowly back up her inner thigh.

His eager tongue was soon parting the soft petals of her own dew-soaked flower, lightly exploring her inner folds. She pictured a butterfly flying from blossom to blossom, its wings catching the light as the colors of joy passed before her closed eyes. Her nectar was flowing freely from her scented blossom.

Gil's thoughts paralleled Jessie's. "I've never smelled a sweeter flower."

"Then pluck me, Gil, pluck me . . ."

Her passion continued to grow until she was no longer certain she could remain in the saddle. She slid forward, into Gil's waiting arms and, in one smooth motion, found herself on her back, surrounded by fragrant blossoms. Gil's face was buried deep in her as he sought out her inflamed bud. He sucked it into his mouth, and Jessie felt her body go rigid. She exploded with intense colors and the world stood still.

Jessie lay there as Gil mounted her. She thought she was numb to more pleasure. Then he slid deep inside of her. And it began again . . .

Ki found the surveyor's shack without any difficulty. He followed the edge of a narrow lake and then at the tip of the western shore spotted the small shack at the mouth of a large meadow. It was a perfect spot, he thought to himself. There was clear water, the lake was brimming with trout, and the field would be home for small game. There was peace here. Ki had often dreamed of such a spot. One day when the battle with the cartel was finished and his duty to Jessie completed, Ki would like such a spot to come to. On the Circle Star he felt very much at home, but it was an adopted home. Eventually he would need to carve out his own place in this new land.

The snow-capped peak that jutted up in the distance and sparkled silver in the fading afternoon light vaguely reminded Ki of a scene from his childhood—a pilgrimage he had taken to Fujiyama when just a youth. That awesome mountain had seemed a thing of magic, a huge jewel in the sky belonging to some spirit. Now, of course, his native land of Japan was distant and unattainable. Ki quickly rid himself of the memories. What was past was best left alone. His many years of training had taught him not only the myriad forms of martial arts but had prepared his mind to deal with the stress and vigors of deadly combat. *Budo,* the way of the warrior, demanded a clear head, unmuddled by emotional attachments to the past. The warrior must freely give of his life; any second thoughts or hesitations would be crippling. Attachments bred fear that the coveted object would eventually be lost. One could not cling to worldly things. And the worst attachment was to that of life itself. Life should be revered, but its loss should never be feared.

The fear of death would have brought disgrace to any of Ki's Japanese ancestors. But Ki was half American and, he said to himself with a smile, only human. He was always striving for inner peace and knew that the road to such was not behind, but ahead. There was no reason to look back. To save himself from drowning in the sorrows of the past he must throw himself into the currents of the present. That meant the railroad, the cartel, the shack, and possible ambush.

On his way up he had watched for any riders on his trail and had even doubled back once to be sure no one was following, but the way was clear. It made little difference; he was certain that the cartel would keep threatening their lives until they were successfully out of the way. And though Ki did not fear death, he didn't feel it should come at the hands of some cartel lackey.

A fair distance from the shack, he slid off the horse and circled around it on foot. It was a quick yet thorough search. No one, man nor beast, had been there in the past few days.

There was nothing more for Ki to do. Jessie and Gil should be arriving shortly, so he decided to start dinner by fashioning a fishing line and heading down to the lake. A trout sizzling in the pan was always a welcome sight, and Ki figured Gil and Jessie would be as hungry as he was. The fish were hungry and biting. Ki returned with three large trout and a story about the big one that got away. He knew it would sound like the typical cliché, but there really was one as big as a saddlebag that jumped right between his legs.

When the fish were scaled and cleaned and the fire was roaring, Ki suddenly realized that the iron cooking pan would scarcely hold one trout let alone three. He thought briefly of skewering the fish on a branch of a young sapling and setting up a spit, but the chance of the delicate meat flaking and falling off into the fire was too great. Instead, Ki walked down to the water's edge and dug up a handful of moist clay. He packed each individual fish with the mud, totally surrounding each with a good two inches.

He poked at the fire, killing most of the flames, and then spread the hot embers out thin. He placed the clay-wrapped fish on the bed of charcoal and then covered them with the rest of the embers. This was an even better way of cooking them. Not knowing exactly when Jessie and Gil were to show up would make it difficult to cook the fish and have it hot but not dried out. Cooking as they were now, though, the fish would remain moist and tender as they steamed inside the clay.

As Ki was relishing the thought of a perfect trout dinner, he heard the distinct crack of a twig. Was he so intent upon his cooking that he had failed to hear someone sneaking up? There was no time for an answer. He rolled quickly to the side and then came up on one knee, *shuriken* in hand.

Ki stared into a pair of cold killer's eyes from a distance of not more than twelve yards and was easy prey. A ragged row of razor-sharp teeth gleamed at Ki. The killer, a large timber wolf, stood ready to pounce. Ki could see the tension in the animal's hindquarters and could hear the animal's low growls become louder and more insistent, but he did not throw his *shuriken*. He would almost surely hit the wolf, for it would take only the merest flick of his wrist to send the throwing star on its way. And the distance between the two would work only to Ki's advantage. Yet he remained there motionless, listening to the animal's guttural snarls.

The timber wolf was large, nearly six feet long, but with his thick coat of silver-tipped fur, it looked even more formidable. Ki could see the animal's rib cage contract with each growl. The wolf sensed danger and was being cautious. Ki was aware that a wrong move, virtually any move, would send the wolf lunging at his throat. It was a question of which would cut the quickest, pointed teeth through human skin or polished metal through animal hide. Ki felt confident of the answer yet hoped he would not have to prove it.

Spittle was dripping down the wolf's long slender tongue, and the animal stopped growling long enough to catch his breath. At no time, though, did he take his eyes off Ki. In this brief moment Ki decided that he wanted to resolve the conflict without resorting to violence. Here in timber country, Ki's attitude toward the beast was different from what he found in Texas. Wolves were major predators and were responsible for the deaths of many cattle. They were hunted regularly, and during periods of bad infestation local cattle associations would offer handsome bounties to rid their lands of the menace. Their pelts, though not as in demand as those of the beaver, would still fetch a fair price. But here there were no cattle to protect, and Ki was not in need of a fur hide. He saw no reason to kill the wolf if it were not necessary, and he did not feel that it would be.

Ki was trained in the art of animal charming, but this tactic was mainly performed on those animals trained for martial purposes. If guards taught an Akita to roam the palace grounds attacking intruders, then ways could be found by those very same intruders to use the dog's own training to control it.

This wolf, however, was not a domesticated animal; there was no previous training that could be utilized to gain mastery over it. There was just natural instinct and the will to survive. Ki hoped a mixture of skill and common sense would avoid a confrontation. The wolf had been attracted to the smell of the dead fish and meant the man no harm. But when Ki spun around on the animal, he was openly challenged and put on his guard. If Ki could relax his own aggressive position and show no fear, the wolf would also relax and ultimately walk away.

Ki slowed his breathing and eased his muscles. He would not think of the animal as a killer, but as a provider. Wolves mated for life, and there was a good chance that this wolf not only had a mate, but had a den of pups to provide for. Ki could not blame the animal for being attracted to the food.

The wolf was quick to pick up on Ki's attitude and soon he stopped growling. Ki then slowly sat back on his heels and placed his hands on the ground. He no longer held the *shuriken*. To do so would have been a hedge and an act of bad faith easily transmitted to the wolf. For the tactic to work, Ki had to be totally sincere. Now that the beast was no longer snarling, it was easy for Ki to find the animal rather beautiful. Beyond the dark gray and silver-tipped fur, there was a well-proportioned head with erect, alert ears. The eyes, now that they had lost their threatening glare, were intelligent and inquisitive. If it were not for wolves being predators and the natural enemies of sheep and cattle, Ki could almost see them as a domesticated breed or at least an animal that could live in close association with man.

Ki was not trying to overpower the wolf, but was trying to deal with him as an equal. Man and beast had now reached a critical point. If, in fact, Ki no longer posed a threat to the wolf, would the animal try to press his advantage and run Ki off? There was nothing to be gained, but wolves were very territorial. Sniffing at the air, the wolf stood up, urinated against the trunk of a tree, marking his territory, and then trotted off.

Ki remained motionless and then broke into a grin. He could imagine the wolf returning to its lair with a story about the big one that got away.

Chapter 9

Jessie was the first to see the rider—his dark form silhouetted against the morning sun as he rode along the sparkling waters of the lake. She set down her tin of hot coffee and shielded her eyes to get a better look. "Any idea who that might be?" she asked as she stood up.

Ki and Gil were also staring at the approaching figure now. "I don't suppose he means us any harm, comin' straight on like he is," Gil said, though his hand slid down to his holstered gun.

"If he's from the camp, he must have been riding for quite some time," Jessie noted aloud.

"And if he's not?" Gil, not being a quick-draw artist, decided to pull his revolver now.

Ki noticed Gil's action. "I wouldn't worry about that, Gil," he stated flatly. "I have a hunch he's a messenger from camp."

"Coming about what?"

"We'll find out in a minute, but I'm sure it won't be good news."

Jessie shot Ki an inquisitive look. Yesterday evening when they reunited, they had exchanged stories and filled each other in over dinner, but she wondered if there were something that he did not want to say in front of Gil. Reluctantly, she turned a suspicious eye on Gil.

Ki sensed her unasked question and shook his head. "No, Jessie, just a hunch," he said to her with a smile. "Their direct attacks have been failures, so it's my guess that they'll now start striking where we're not, trying to keep us off balance."

"Well, if he's bringing bad news, it's a good thing for him these are modern days." She gestured to the rider and tried to sound more jovial than she felt. "In ancient times the bearer of bad news didn't have a very propitious future."

Ki could feel their collective good mood vanish quickly. Last night, after formulating a makeshift plan that centered on the Oregon Central, they had gone to bed with a glimmer of hope. Jessie was certain an investigation would link the railroad directly to the cartel, and then they would have a clear target. They would retaliate as often as necessary to force the cartel into submission. The cartel would either stop its attacks on the Wood River or the Oregon Central would be brought to ruin. As Jessie had said, "Two can play this game."

But now their positive attitude was fast slipping away. There could be no retaliation if Jessie and Ki were constantly kept on the run dealing with disasters and chasing phantoms. The true nature of sabotage was rearing its ugly head. There were not only the physical damage and the possible loss of life to contend with, but the debilitating effects on morale. And in the long run, Ki felt the insidious side effects were all the more dangerous and destructive.

This was all without knowing for certain the nature of the messenger's business. But they would know shortly. Over the last hundred yards, the rider had spurred his horse into a gallop and was soon reining the sweaty gelding to a halt.

"Miss Starbuck, got a message for you," the rider said as he caught his breath. "Been riding most the night." He didn't sound happy about it.

Jessie stretched out her hand, "Well?"

"Oh, yeah." Still mounted, he reached into his shirt pocket, pulled out a folded paper, and handed it to her. "Spike figured you'd be up here surveyin'. He said if I waited till morning you'd probably have pulled up stakes."

"Lighten your saddle and pour yourself some coffee," Jessie said as she unfolded the telegram. "There's a biscuit or two if you'd like," she continued. Then she began to read the message. Ki watched her face carefully, and though she tried to conceal her emotions, he could easily see her anger and frustration. She took a deep breath, then folded the telegram, and stuffed it into her jacket pocket.

"Gil, there's been some trouble at the Starbuck lumber mill. We'll have to be heading back." She turned to Ki and, in a lower voice, told him, "In a former life you must have been a master strategist." She patted her jacket pocket. "You called this one right." There was a twinkle in her eye that Ki found reassuring.

Gil moved to saddle his horse, as did Jessie and Ki. The messenger seemed to be eyeing the activity with an air of indifference, though he did keep a watchful eye on Ki. They were soon ready to hit the trail and Gil turned to the messenger. "Kick some dirt on the fire, and let's head out."

The man turned a belligerent face to Gil. "Spike said I could—"

"I don't care what Spike said!" Gil cut the man short. "The Wood River ain't paying you to loll in the sun."

The man rose to his feet slowly. "What's your name?" Gil inquired. "I don't recall seeing your face."

"Schmitt, track layer. Just signed on."

"I'm Gil Johnson, chief locator. What I say goes. There'll be time to rest later. You'll get what's coming to you."

Ki had been studying Schmitt, a short, husky man with dark hair. He had the build of a track layer, but he did not move like one. He was arrogant, yet did not back up his threats with his physical mass. Most laborers were quick to support their threats with a body gesture that would convey their strength and muscle. But Schmitt's stance was arrogant and lazy. It was almost as if he had something better than plain muscle to back up his threats—something perhaps that would spit fire, pump lead, and leave a man face down and cold. Ki was certain the man was used to wearing a six-shooter, and from the almost imperceptibly worn area on the outside hip of his pants, Ki judged Schmitt was also accustomed to wearing his gun low. And although Ki hadn't gotten a good look yet, he was positive a close inspection of this track layer's hands wouldn't show more than a callus or two.

They rode hard, but kept from pushing the horses beyond their limits. For the most part they traveled in silence, exchanging only pleasantries. Jessie would have liked the opportunity to talk to Ki alone, but that was not possible. She was at the front, and Ki was bringing up the rear, no doubt keeping a sharp eye on Schmitt. She also realized that any time their movements were predictable, as they were now, they were fair game for an ambush. She focused her attention far ahead. It would do no good to spot an ambush after they walked into it, she thought bemusedly.

They stopped briefly at noon to rest the horses and had a quick trail lunch from what Pops had given Ki. As they mounted, Gil held Jessie's horse steady. It was an unnecessary gesture, but it gave him a moment alone with her.

"Jessie, I'd like to help. If there's anything I can do . . . if you want me to go out there with you . . ."

"Thanks, Gil," she said with a smile, "but your place is with the railroad. One way to beat the cartel is to finish this line as fast as possible. You take care of that and I'll handle this trouble."

"Be careful, Jessie, please." She nodded to him and he let go of the reins and mounted his own horse.

• • •

Just after dinner they pulled into camp. They headed straight for Spike's tent. The surly foreman was stretched out on his cot, a bottle of whiskey at his side. Liquor was strictly prohibited in camp, but Spike made no attempt to hide the bottle. He removed a foul cigar from his mouth and rolled it between his fingers. "So you got the message; good work, Schmitt."

"There any other word?" Jessie asked immediately.

"From the mill? No." Spike shook his head.

Jessie turned to Gil. "Can we get fresh mounts?" Then she addressed Ki, "How do you feel?"

"Ready."

"I guess you folks'll be wanting to move out as fast as possible," Spike said as he swung his legs to the floor and sat up. There was little concern in his voice. He continued, "I got a work train heading out first thing in the morning. It'd be worth your while to spend the night and ride it down the line."

"He's right, Jessie," Gil was quick to add.

Spike suppressed a nasty grin. "You can take it as far as Gilman's Crossing. From there you can ride a half day to the Oregon Central. That'll take you right out to the coast."

At the mention of the other railroad, Jessie and Gil exchanged wary glances.

Spike let out a disagreeable chuckle. "I hate to send the competition any business, but this is an emergency."

A thought struck Jessie. "I'd like someone to come along with us," she said and paused. Then she added, "Maybe Schmitt."

Both Schmitt and Spike seemed taken aback. Schmitt started to protest, but was cut off by Spike, who held up his hand. "Ain't possible," he said gruffly. "We're short-handed as it is."

"He just signed on the other day. You won't miss him that much."

Schmitt began complaining again. "I've done about all the traveling I care to do. I didn't sign on to nursemaid no lady!"

Jessie wheeled on him. "You signed on to do a day's work, mister, and I decide what work you do."

Schmitt turned to appeal to Spike, "You hired me to—"

Jessie cut him off short. "Spike may have hired you, but I can darn well fire you!" She stared directly at the foreman.

"You can't talk to my men like that."

"Commodore Whiting gave me full authority to do damn well what I please. And if you don't like it, McCaully, you can hit the trail now."

Jessie gave the man time to respond. They had confronted each other the first day she arrived, but apparently Spike had to be put in his place periodically. When Spike said nothing, she turned to Schmitt. "Be ready first thing tomorrow."

After Jessie's outburst, Schmitt didn't feel like opening his mouth, but his eyes were pleading to Spike.

"Could you take someone else?" Spike asked almost humbly. "Schmitt's had a hard ride."

Jessie's voice was calm and understanding, yet she remained firm. "I'd like to keep the situation hushed. The fewer who know about it the better. Schmitt knows, so he goes. He'll be rested by morning." She turned and left. There was nothing more to be said.

The next morning the sun did not seem to rise. Heavy gray clouds stretched across the sky, blotting out most of the light. What little did creep through was flat and featureless and turned the landscape into a shadowless panorama of muted grays. The trees, the sky, the boxcars all melded together, practically indistinguishable from each other. The mountain peaks, always so crisply outlined against the powder-blue sky, were lost in the mist. Moisture hung heavy in the air and one could see as well as feel the tiny droplets.

It promised to be a cold, bleak day, but Ki stepped out from Gil's caboose smiling and refreshed. Gil had offered to pitch another tent, but Ki told him it was unnecessary, he'd sleep in a boxcar. But once Gil and Jessie went to bed down in the mess tent, Ki went calling on Miss Cynthia. For the night, he set aside thoughts of sabotage and the cartel. Without some diversion the anger and frustration would fester and blacken his soul. He sought a balance, something good and wholesome to offset the evil of the cartel. Cynthia was as far from evil as one could get and, Ki thought to himself with a smile, such a lovely diversion. The day might be gloomy; Ki's spirits were anything but.

The camp was just beginning to stir, and things were still relatively quiet. On his way to the mess tent, he heard angry voices coming from Spike's tent. He was too distant to make out the words, but he had a hunch the two men engaged in conversation were Schmitt and the foreman. A few quick, silent steps took him to the side of the tent.

"You'll do as you're told!" Ki heard Spike say sharply. Apparently, Schmitt was still trying to get out of making the trip.

"I can always quit. You can't make me do nothin'," Schmitt whined.

There was a brief pause, and Ki could imagine Spike sitting there chomping on the end of his stogie. "No one is makin' you do nothin', Schmitt," Spike said with a deceptive warmth. "You just turn and leave here and forget you ever laid eyes on me. Just don't come crawlin' back on your belly!" From the foreman's tone, there was little doubt that Schmitt was backed into a corner and had no choice but to do as Spike said. There was no reply from Schmitt. Spike continued, "Good. Go grab some coffee and get on the work train."

Suddenly, the tent flap flew open and Schmitt stormed out. Ki was crouched down low to avoid being noticed, but the man never even turned around. Had Ki gotten there just a minute earlier, he might have uncovered something important, but as it was the exchange he overheard told him little he didn't already know. Schmitt was not precisely what he made himself out to be and, for some reason, was very reluctant to make the trip with him and Jessie. Spike was already under suspicion, but this conversation exposed nothing substantial. But given time, all would be revealed.

Ki took Spike's advice himself and grabbed some hot coffee before heading up to the train. When he got there, Gil was at the last car saying good-bye to Jessie.

"I hope everything works out," Gil said as his hands fidgeted with his Stetson.

"It will," Jessie assured him. "You just keep pushing the tracks westward, young man," she said with a smile.

"This afternoon I'm heading out with a crew to start building the last trestle. When you get back, it'll be finished and we'll be through the pass."

"I hope so."

"You can count on it," Gil said as he gave her a formal bow. The train whistle let out a shrill *toot* as the engineer checked the steam pressure. "You better get onboard."

"Bye, Gil." She would have liked to have said more, but this was not the time or the place. The nights they'd shared together would have to speak for themselves. She climbed up the iron stairs and stood on the outside platform of the car.

There was a longer blast from the whistle and then with a lurch the train began to roll forward. Ki took a running step and hopped onboard beside Jessie.

"Schmitt?" he asked.

She nodded and pointed a thumb over her shoulder. "He's sitting inside and looking none too happy about it."

Ki nodded and then turned to go inside. Jessie grabbed him by the arm. "Wait a minute, Ki. I want to show you something." She reached into her pocket and pulled out the message. "Read this," she said and handed him the paper.

In a very neat, stylish handwriting was the following message:

EMERGENCY—BIG FIRE—SUSPICIOUS—ALL WORK HALTED—COME IMMEDIATELY
ED LARSON

She gave him a moment to read it and then asked, "What do you think?" But before Ki could respond, she stated plainly, "It's as phony as a wooden nickel."

"I'm suspicious, too, Jessie, but what makes you so sure?"

"Look at it. How many emergency messages have you received written in such a fine hand? They are usually scrawled."

"It makes sense," Ki said. Then he told her of his suspicions.

Jessie nodded her head. "I think it's time to find out what Mr. Schmitt knows."

"We'll have to rein him in slowly, Jessie."

"We'll break him like a bucking bronc," she said with a confident smile.

Ki had no doubts that she would do just that.

In the empty Pullman car, Schmitt was sitting by the window, unhappily watching the passing scenery. Jessie went to the seat in front of him and turned it around so she could sit facing him. Without a word, Schmitt stretched out his legs and placed his boots on the seat directly opposite him.

Unfazed, Jessie sat down catty-cornered from him and began to strike up a friendly conversation. "Think it'll rain later in the day?" Schmitt ignored the question. He held Jessie personally responsible for dragging him along on this trip. "In these parts they say the sun often burns off the haze by midday," she continued. "You from around here, Schmitt?" There was still no response, but it didn't matter. She was laying the groundwork and would get around to everything in good time. "Awfully nice country up here, much different from Texas, where Ki and I are from." She gestured to Ki, who was sitting across the aisle.

The reference to Ki had Schmitt readjusting his sitting

position. Jessie smiled to herself. Just the mention of Ki seemed to make Schmitt a little nervous; Jessie decided to play on that. "I don't mind the rain, but Ki likes dry weather. He gets pretty darn ornery when he gets wet." There was a thinly veiled threat that, judging by the look in his eyes, Schmitt had been quick to pick up. Jessie then softened her tone. "But I say the rain makes the flowers grow, so it's all fine with me. Right where we were camped there was this exquisite field of wildflowers—"

Finally Schmitt could stand no more of this idle chatter. "Look, lady, you can make me ride this damn train, but you can't make me be sociable. You wanna pratter, do it with your Chinaman!" He mumbled a few sharp words to himself and then added out loud, "I don't want no part of this, you hear?"

Here was the opening Jessie was waiting for. "I'm sorry to hear that, Schmitt—since we're all in this together." That caught his attention. "When a ship goes down, everyone on it better start swimming."

"I don't know what you're talkin' about," Schmitt said. He turned to stare out the window, but there was an edge of fear in his voice.

Jessie let him be, allowing time for the fear to fester and spread. It was important to crack Schmitt and find out everything he knew. It would be a waiting game, and time was not necessarily on Jessie's side, but she could almost see the apprehension growing in Schmitt. As the miles passed by, he became more and more restless, fidgeting first with his hat and then with a dark blue bandanna that he had pulled from his shirt pocket.

The train began to slow and Schmitt looked even more worried. Ki got up to see if they were stopping, but on his way out, he leaned over to Schmitt and said in a low ominous voice, "When a rattler strikes, it doesn't stop to look whose leg it's biting."

They had pulled into a small depot and were apparently taking on water. Ki felt like stretching his legs, but did not know how long a stop they would be making, so he did not venture far. He walked up the length of the train, a half dozen empty coal cars being shipped back for refills. It did seem like a waste, the constant need to ship empty freight cars, but as Gil had told both him and Jessie, it was a problem that no one had yet been able to solve, though many railroads found themselves in financial trouble for not considering the added expense of such runs. All too often a poorly run road would not have proper budgeting and planning and would wind up with an excess of empty cars at the end of the line.

Ki was drawn from his thoughts by a movement on the other side of the train. He ducked down under the cars to take a look, but he saw nothing. He started to climb through the space between cars when the train whistle sounded. He scurried back to the coach car. It was probably just the engineer or brakeman climbing aboard. It might even have been a prairie dog scampering into its hole. He didn't give it another thought.

The engine slowly picked up speed, but in the coach the battle of nerves was continuing at full speed. From the beads of sweat that were forming on Schmitt's brow, it was a fair bet that he was close to cracking.

"Ki, what time do you reckon we'll be pulling in to Gilman's Crossing?" Jessie asked. It was obviously a rhetorical question, designed to rankle Schmitt's frazzled nerves, and Ki didn't bother to answer. "My, at this rate, even with another water stop, it shouldn't take long at all. Then, with any luck, we'll be at the mill two days after next."

Suddenly, something struck Ki, and it was triggered by Jessie's saying "with any luck." It would take luck, probably more luck than either of them had. The message was a fake, and both Jessie and Ki suspected that it was a ploy to remove them from the scene. But what about Schmitt's unease about making the trip. He was just following orders. In his role as messenger, he wouldn't know that the message was a phony. And even with Ki's reputation as the Pinkerton,

Schmitt could always play dumb and would have nothing to fear—unless, of course, there was a play to remove Jessie and Ki permanently. And this, Ki realized unhappily, was the perfect setup. The cartel would know where they were every step of the way. There would be no mistake here. There wasn't even another car for them to go to. If an ambush were planned, that would explain Schmitt's nervousness.

"Jessie, I have a hunch we're being herded to market."

Jessie immediately caught his drift. She turned to Schmitt and asked him outright, "There any truth to that?" Schmitt looked uneasily from Ki to Jessie, but said nothing. "Maybe you don't realize who you're dealing with, but Spike and his kind won't hesitate to get rid of you along with us. Your kind comes cheap, Schmitt. As long as they get us, they don't give a plugged nickel as to what becomes of you!"

"I don't know about me, but your hide ain't worth a plugged nickel." His words were tough, but his faltering, dry voice showed how scared he really was.

"Don't you realize that whatever happens to us, you'll probably get the same?"

Schmitt swallowed hard, his eyes bulging slightly. "I think he realizes just that, Jessie." Ki's tone was not harsh. "Our Mr. Schmitt is caught in a stampede and there's no way out." Just then Ki remembered that which had caught his attention back at the water stop. He jumped to his feet and raced to the back of the car. "Keep him covered," he instructed Jessie, then opened the door, and stepped out on the platform. He leaned over both sides and looked down the outside length of the Pullman coach.

There was no need for an ambush when an easily lobbed stick of TNT would do the trick. He was a fool not to realize it.

He placed a foot up on the metal railing and grabbed hold of the overhanging roof. With the swaying and unexpected lurches of the train, he took extra precautions before swinging himself up to the roof.

As he pulled himself up, he caught sight of a man coming his way from the far end of the train. As Ki got up, the other man dropped into the first of the empty cars. Ki thought the man was carrying something in his hand, something long and cylindrical. Ki couldn't be certain but it seemed as if that something might be a stick of TNT.

Chapter 10

Ki was pretty sure he had not been noticed. The suspect had dropped down about the same time Ki stood up and he was probably concentrating on his balance. Experience had taught Ki that most men had a tendency to look down and not up. That meant the element of surprise was Ki's. All he had to do was get to the man before he got too near the caboose.

Ki moved as swiftly as he dared. With one wrong step, he could be thrown from the train. To maintain his advantage and to continue to remain undetected, he would have to make it across the roof of the coach before the man climbed into the next coal car. He lowered his body into a crouch, but kept his back upright and straight. This put tremendous strain on his thigh muscles, but it lowered his center of gravity significantly without hindering his freedom of movement. In essence, his powerful legs were acting as huge springs, absorbing the jostling and lurching of the train. From a distance he looked as if he were riding an imaginary horse.

Before he took a step or lifted his foot, he would make

sure his other foot was firmly planted. His weight was never shifted until both feet were securely placed. To a layman all this would seem to hinder speedy progress, but to Ki moving this way was second nature, and done just as a mountain lion stalks its prey.

In no time Ki found himself at the end of the roof. It was an easy drop to the extended front platform of the Pullman, and from there Ki could easily cross over to the last of the coal cars. It would not be difficult to climb up and over the side of the coal tender, but there was a risk involved. From his lower position between cars, Ki could not be certain where the other man was. It was possible that as Ki was climbing up and over, the man would be doing the same. Discovery in that case would be all too certain, and it was crucial that Ki continue undetected. The cartel tough could have any number of dynamite sticks, against which Ki was virtually defenseless. One stick would easily remove Ki from the picture; the next stick could be used to blow up Jessie and the coach car.

There was only one thing to do. Ki would have to jump across and into the coal car. The distance, only about four feet, was not much of a problem, but Ki had to be sure that his momentum would carry him far enough. Rather than take a few steps back for a running jump, Ki decided it would be faster to dive head first into the coal car. The man might pop up at any time. Ki just hoped that the bottom of the coal tender was clean and flat enough to enable him to tuck and roll to his feet safely.

But without another thought, Ki bent his powerful legs and sprang forward. Looking down, he saw the tender wall pass by, and then a moment before he struck the floor of the car, he tucked his chin to his chest and covered his head with his arms. His forearms, as hard as a seasoned plank of wood, were the first to make contact with the metal floor. But his forward momentum had him rolling over and the impact was quickly distributed over the mass of his sinewy back. He rolled rapidly to his feet.

He rushed to the far end of the car and hesitated. Where was the man? Was he planning to place the dynamite on the coach car and detonate it with a long fuse or would he use a short fuse and lob it into the Pullman from a few cars back? Ki couldn't take the risk of trying to outguess him; he had to prepare himself for either eventuality. If the man were planning to toss the TNT, he would be in good throwing range even one more car back. But Ki reasoned he wouldn't throw it blind; he would climb up on the edge of the car to toss the dynamite. That would give Ki the opportunity to hit the man with a *shuriken* just before the toss. But if the cartel tough managed to light the dynamite, even if he couldn't throw it, the explosion would derail the train and cause serious injuries.

Ki continued to run the alternatives through his head. He could sit atop the edge of the car waiting for the man to show just the very top of his head. The *shuriken* could be thrown with enough velocity to embed itself deep enough to kill him instantly. Ki would be allowed only a very small margin of error. Normally that would not have bothered him, but there were the unexpected lurches of the speeding train to contend with, and Ki did not want to have to depend on something beyond his control—at least not now.

The best alternative was to meet the cartel man in hand-to-hand combat, but that meant that Ki would have to risk exposure one last time and climb over the wall and into the next car. There was really no other good alternative. Ki jumped up, grasped the top of the wall, and pulled himself up and over. Then, as he stood on the car coupling about to climb up into the next car, he realized he was now ideally situated. It was a precarious location; the coupling was narrow and did not offer a very secure footing, but Ki felt that that was a slight drawback when weighed against the advantages.

No matter what the thug intended to do, he would be climbing over the wall that Ki now rested against. Even if he were planning to throw the TNT from here, he would have to hook a leg over the edge for balance. And that was when he would be most vulnerable. A quick and unexpected yank from Ki would easily topple the stunned man. He could imagine the man's shock and the surprise on his face as he felt the first tug on his leg. A smile formed on Ki's lips. If it weren't such a deadly game, it would be funny.

Ki flattened his back against the wall and stretched out his leg, wedging it against the adjoining car. It was a moderately stable position, but Ki reckoned he wouldn't have long to wait. He was right.

Only moments later he heard the sound of boots hitting the metal wall. The thug was using his feet to help climb the side. Ki stood ready. Any second the leg would swing over. But much to Ki's surprise, he suddenly found himself staring directly up into a puffy, red face. The man, looking right at a crouching and ready Ki, opened his mouth in a startled cry and exhibited a row of broken, tobacco-stained teeth. Ki had used the strength of his arms to swing his legs nimbly over the wall, and he expected the cartel tough to do likewise. But apparently the sheer weight of the man dictated a different maneuver. The portly thug pulled and kicked his torso over the top, and then, resting his wide girth on the edge, he leaned far forward from his waist in order to swing his legs over the top.

After the initial surprise of having the man's face so close to his, Ki responded much the same. Instead of yanking on a leg, Ki grabbed a lockful of hair with one hand and the back of the collar with the other. The man was so poorly balanced that it took no more effort to bring him down than it would a sack of potatoes.

The thug's feet swung over the top and his head fell down against the base of the car with a resounding crack that Ki could hear even above the rattling of the train. The man was knocked unconscious, and Ki was in immediate danger of being knocked from his position by the slumping tub of lard. He acted quickly—simultaneously kicking at the body that lay at his feet while jumping over it and grabbing hold of the top edge of the wall.

The man rolled from between the cars and down to the side of the track bed. He was fortunate not to have fallen between the cars and been ground to a pulp by the wheels. Ki half suspected that the man's formidable size saved him from such a grizzly end. The man was simply too fat to fit. But judging from the red streak that ran down the base of the coupler, it was questionable whether the thug would survive or bleed to death along the right of way.

It mattered little to Ki. Jessie was safe and that was the end of it. The man was a cold-blooded, hired killer. Ki felt no remorse.

When Ki re-entered the coach, Jessie was sitting across the aisle from Schmitt, her .38 pointing directly at him.

"What happened, Ki?" Jessie asked, her gun never moving off Schmitt.

"A cartel lackey, heading this way with a fistful of dynamite." He slid into the seat behind Schmitt.

There was no need for Jessie to ask what became of him. Ki would not have returned until the threat was disposed of. But the ramification of the act hit her instantly. "Instead of sending us on a wild-goose chase, as I first thought, they were really planning a one-way trip for us."

Ki nodded. "They mean business," he stated tersely.

Jessie directed her next comment to Schmitt. "That should leave you no doubt where you stand. They were throwing you to the dogs, Schmitt." Her voice had a cruel rasp to it. "I think it's time for you to do a little talking."

"I don't know nothin' about this. Honest, I don't. You gotta believe me," he said as he wiped the sweat off his forehead.

"I think he's too scared to be lying, Jessie," Ki said as he studied their captive.

"It's true, ma'am." Schmitt's eyes darted pleadingly from Jessie to Ki. His belligerent tone was now completely gone.

"What was he doing while I was gone?" Ki asked.

"Staring out the window and looking like a sick pup."

Jessie thought a moment and then lowered her gun. She no longer felt it was necessary. "I guess you're right," she continued. "If I knew they were planning to blow up this car, I'd try anything to get out. But there's still a lot to learn from him."

The sudden realization that he was truly expendable in the cartel's eyes changed Schmitt's attitude instantly. "I don't know much; I'm just a hired gun."

"Hired to do what?" Jessie asked.

"Ride out and deliver the message, no questions asked."

"You don't know anything about the cartel?" Jessie felt a little foolish asking, but felt she had to.

"The what?" Schmitt replied.

"Never mind. Who hired you?"

"Don't know his name. Never even saw him."

"Then how'd you get hitched on?" Jessie persisted.

"I got into some trouble in Basin City and—"

Jessie interrupted him. "Basin City—is that where the Oregon Central runs?"

Schmitt nodded. "It was originally just a railroad depot, but it wasn't long before the town grew—"

"What kind of trouble were you in?" Jessie interrupted him once again.

"It was at the poker table. This slicker was dealing me dirt, and when I called him on it, he went for a derringer he kept in his lap. I was just a bit faster, though, and beat him to it. But I wasn't so sure the law would see it so clearly—me drillin' him like that. Then this stocky fella comes up and tells me he'll take care of everything if I can just do him a favor. Says he's lookin' for some good men who ain't afraid of some shootin'. Seein' as how I didn't have no choice in the matter, I went along. And that's all I know."

Jessie's next question, one about the stocky man, was cut short by a sudden jar as the train rounded a bend. "Ki, what do you think that was?"

"I don't know, but I intend to find out," he said as he

stood up and began to walk to the front of the car. He stepped out, but saw nothing suspicious.

"There might have been a small obstacle on the track, a rabbit perhaps," Ki announced as he stepped back in.

Jessie nodded. "That must have been it; things seem fine now."

"Then again, I don't know all there is to know about railroading," Ki added.

The train was creeping its way up a long grade and was steadily losing speed. When the coach slowed to practically a standstill, Jessie's concerned look returned. "Ki, this doesn't seem right," she said with a strong emphasis.

Ki raced to the front platform of the coach car. He could hear the locomotive, but the train was not moving. A moment later he did feel a slight movement; it was backward. Listening closely, he realized that the sound of the steam engine was slowly fading in the distance.

To confirm his fears, he rushed back through the car to the rear platform. By that time the car was definitely rolling backward and picking up speed. A tight turn loomed in the distance. By the time the runaway cars hit the bend they would jump the tracks and go plummeting down the precipice that now bordered the tracks.

Ki rushed into the coach. "Jessie, quick! We have to get off the train!"

There was an urgency in his voice that Jessie knew not to question. Experience had taught her to trust Ki's judgment. When Ki said duck, she ducked; when he said run, she ran. She stood up and followed Ki out to the back of the car. At the door she realized that Schmitt was frozen in his seat. She called out to him, "Come on!" Schmitt turned to her slowly as if in a daze.

"Jessie, we don't have much time," Ki said urgently.

"We can't leave him here."

Ki stepped back inside. "Schmitt!" he yelled sharply. "Move!" The mention of his name seemed to galvanize Schmitt into action—that and Jessie's tug on his arm. Together, Jessie and Ki rushed the frightened man down the aisle and out to the platform.

The curve was coming closer every second, and the ground beneath them was speeding by faster and faster. Schmitt, panicked by the rush of movement, gripped the handrail tightly.

"Don't look down at the ground," warned Ki. "Pick out a tree and lock your eyes on it." Schmitt was too far gone to heed the advice, but Ki continued giving hurried instructions. "Jump as far as you can. Stay loose. Don't tense up. Wrap your arms around you. When you hit the ground, just let yourself roll."

Ki turned to look at the approaching curve. They were running out of time. "Ready, Schmitt?" There was no response, but Ki did not expect one. He stood behind Schmitt and placed one hand gently on the terrified man's back. The other he placed around Jessie's waist.

"Jump!" He gave Schmitt a gentle push and then wrapped his arms protectively around Jessie before diving off the platform. He made one mistake, though—underestimating the man's fear and strength. Ki's push was enough to get Schmitt started, but not enough to break the hold he had on the railing. Schmitt held tenaciously to the iron bar, refusing to let go even after Ki's push sent him off the platform.

Ki saw Schmitt's body swing off the platform in an arc that sent him crashing against the back of the car. He didn't let go and the last thing Ki saw was Schmitt dangling from the rear of the platform. There was no need to see more. It was all too obvious what would happen next. Either Schmitt would continue to hang on until the car jumped the tracks or he would lose his grip and fall underneath the wheels of the runaway car. It didn't really matter; either was a gory end.

Ki was careful to hit the ground on his side, so he would be in the best position to absorb much of the shock of the landing and not crush Jessie, whom he still held tightly in his arms. They had come down far enough away from the gravel and the ground was soft and covered with fallen boughs. After four quick rolls, the two bodies were still.

Jessie sat up, smiling, and looked around at the tall pines that surrounded them. "We're lucky we didn't hit a tree," she said.

"You're okay?" Ki asked with concern.

"Yes. But I wouldn't want to have to do it again." She was lighthearted about it, but after looking around, she didn't see Schmitt and her tone changed. "Where's Schmitt?" she asked, afraid she already knew the answer.

Ki was shaking his head. "He didn't make it," he said sadly.

"Are you sure?"

"I didn't see the body, but I'm sure. He didn't let go, Jessie. He didn't have a chance."

"Damn!" Jessie rarely used profane language. She had to be really upset.

"Despite his last minute change of heart, he was still a killer," Ki said in an effort to console her.

"I know that, Ki, but there was more he had to tell us."

"I don't want you feeling too sorry for him," Ki said somewhat sheepishly.

That brought a smile back to Jessie's face. "I'm not feeling sorry for him, Ki. I'm feeling sorry for all the innocent people who will get hurt if we can't stop the cartel."

Ki nodded in understanding, then stood up, and offered Jessie his hand.

"Mind if we just sit a spell, Ki?"

"Of course not," he said as he sat down. "It's not like we have any pressing engagements."

"Now, what was all this about?"

"I'm not sure, but I have a pretty good idea."

"Well, go ahead."

"The thug with the dynamite must have had a partner on the train. When there was no explosion, the partner probably thought his friend had lost his balance and had fallen from the train. The man was quite fat, so there was a good chance that might have happened. The partner moved back a few cars and then waited for the right time to uncouple the cars."

"That was that first jolt we felt."

"Right. On that bit of winding track, the runaway coach was an almost certain deathtrap."

"Well, it was for Schmitt." The thought brought back Jessie's anger and frustration. "Every time we start getting somewhere, we wind up back where we started," she said as she sullenly poked a twig into the ground.

"That's not totally true, Jessie."

"We learn a tad more, but we're still on the defensive," argued Jessie. "We still don't know where or when the cartel is going to strike next."

"It's important to make sure the cartel isn't successful, no matter where or when they strike."

"That's just it, Ki; it's a cat-and-mouse game, and I'm tired of always being the mouse!"

"The more we know, the better chance we have."

"We have to get the upper hand soon. What do you suggest, Ki?"

"We can't be far from Gilman's Crossing. I can get a horse and ride into Basin City. If I can find that stocky fellow who hired Schmitt—"

"But we don't know anything about him, not even his name," Jessie interrupted.

"I don't think it'll be that difficult. I plan to let him find me."

"Then let's get started," Jessie said as she stood.

"It might be best if I go alone, posing as a vagabond rail laborer."

"We wouldn't have to go in together, I could—"

Ki was already shaking his head. "An unescorted woman might raise questions, and questions are what we want to avoid."

"I guess you're right, Ki. Strangers, especially pretty ones, do tend to raise a few eyebrows." Jessie wasn't boasting, just talking from experience. There were times in the past when her very appearance caused enough of a stir to hinder the investigations they had planned. "I wouldn't want to blow our best shot. I think I'll head back to the camp—maybe give a look at the depots along the way."

"I was going to suggest just that, Jessie. I'll feel better knowing you're at the railhead keeping an eye on things."

Jessie realized Ki was probably being tactful by refraining from mentioning the other side of the coin. "You sure you don't mean you'd feel better knowing that I was safe and sound among friends?" she asked teasingly.

"I think I can count on you taking pretty fair care of yourself." Ki could be certain of that; he had trained her personally. He did not like to leave her, but when he did, he could usually trust her to handle herself well.

"Thanks." She rose to her feet. "Well, good luck, Ki."

"And despite what I said, you be careful, too." The smile on his face did not undercut the care in his voice. He turned and took off into the woods.

Chapter 11

The day was still overcast and misty, but the chill in the air was gone. Jessie followed the tracks back the way they had come. In the coach car, she had been too occupied with Schmitt to take notice of the land. For the most part, the tracks ran through thick timberland. The soft daylight reflected the deep greens and earthy browns of the lush pine forest. Earlier in the day it had probably rained here, for Jessie could smell the thick aroma of wet ground and fresh evergreens.

Her idle pratter with Schmitt had some truth; she did appreciate rain. From a totally pragmatic standpoint most Texas cattle ranchers appreciated rain; it was necessary for their herds. Nothing would cause more anxiety than a prolonged dry spell. Not only would watering holes dry up, but grazing land would also suffer, sometimes to the extent that the grass wouldn't grow back for at least another season.

But Jessie appreciated the rain for other less practical reasons. There was a feeling here, as she went through the damp woods, that one couldn't experience on the prairies or rolling plains of Texas. Texas was a tough, unforgiving land, hard and crisp, but still very beautiful. Jessie couldn't think of anything more pleasing than a late summer sunset on the range back home. But these northern timberlands had an appeal all their own. They were lush and comforting, almost maternal and feminine compared to the rugged, manly expanse of Texas.

Her footsteps were muffled in the rich soil that bordered the roadbed, and her anger and frustration slowly evaporated in the hours she spent walking in peaceful solitude.

The tracks she had followed passed over numerous streams and gullies, but now she came to a giant gorge that stopped her in her tracks. Jessie found it hard to judge the height of the railroad trestle that spanned it—so captivated was she by the rushing waters that passed under it. It could have been anywhere from one hundred to two hundred feet, but probably somewhere in the middle.

She crossed the trestle slowly so that she could study the clear waters below her. Looking down between the railroad ties placed a frame around her field of vision. It was almost like looking at a fine work of art, a magic painting, one capable of movement. And each step changed the picture. Sometimes she would step back and compare, or she would rush ahead and watch as the pictures under her blended into one.

She had another fanciful thought: a great museum filled with these magical pictures. She could hear the sound of the rushing waters, and that made everything even better. Movement and sound. She had been to the great museums of Europe and had seen great works of art, but she had never seen anything as special as this.

When she suddenly found herself across the bridge, it was not without a bit of disappointment. Looking back at the gorge, she realized that, although she had traveled virtually all over the world, she had never come across as much natural beauty as right here in her own country. There were, of course, places of beauty elsewhere, but no other country could seemingly offer such a spectacular range of radiant splendor.

Then, just as suddenly, she thought of the cartel that was trying to get control of all this—the cartel whose greed would pollute the spirit of America. Jessie turned away from the gorge. Some other time perhaps she could stand here and watch the flowing waters, some other time when there was not a blight of evil hanging over the land and fouling the air. She quickened her pace; there was a job to get done.

She made good progress and was somewhat startled to find herself within sight of the water depot. She was also surprised to see four horses tethered outside the small shack. With a train already having passed through and no other in sight, there would be no reason for honest men to be there, Jessie realized instantly. She immediately left the tracks and darted into the woods, using the trees to cover her.

When she reached the edge of the woods and was just about to cross the open right of way, the door of the shack opened and two husky men stepped out. One was short and bald with heavy jowls; Jessie remembered seeing him in the camp. The other, a bit taller with a dirty beard, Jessie didn't recall seeing before. Her hand automatically went to her holster; then she cursed softly. There was nothing there.

She couldn't believe it. It must have fallen out when they jumped from the train. She could almost recall the jar that might have knocked it loose. Schmitt's death, the loss of their one good lead, had put her in such a tizzy she had failed to realize her revolver had slipped from her holster. Then, her solitary walk had lulled her into her own private world where the loss of her gun continued unnoticed. Now, she had only her derringer. Thinking of her .38 Colt made her curse softly again. Granted, the six-shooter was very special to her, a gift given to her by her father, and was a very beautiful piece of work, but right now what concerned her more was the need for a fast-shooting accurate weapon. She hung back behind the tree and reconsidered her options.

With her Colt it would have been easy to get the drop on these two. In fact, she had intended to do just that in order to wring any bit of information out of them, but now she had to rethink her plans. But when the two men mounted and rode off, taking the other two horses with them, Jessie immediately decided on a plan of action.

She waited a respectable amount of time for the riders to disappear and then made her way down to the shack. She moved quickly and cagily, though stealth was not necessary to her plan. Even if she were spotted, a lone woman would not be considered much of a threat. But that—Jessie smiled to herself at the thought—had been the downfall of more than one overconfident man.

However, she did steer clear of the small window on the front side of the building. She pushed open the door and stepped inside quickly. At the sound of the door the depot attendant turned. He was young, about eighteen, and this was probably his first job. A look of surprise crossed his face and then he reached for his gun. But Jessie already had her arm extended, her derringer trained dead on the mark.

"This is a tiny weapon, mister," she said bluntly. "I may have to put two holes into your forehead!" The young man lowered his gun. "Put it on the floor, butt first," Jessie instructed. "Now kick it over, easy."

The attendant did as he was told, but kept looking past her shoulder. Jessie smiled. "Your friends are long gone," she told him flatly. "Don't expect any help." She bent and picked up the .44 caliber revolver.

"I don't have any money," the attendant blurted out. He continued to look around nervously, and Jessie finally caught on.

"It's just little ole me," she informed him good-naturedly. Apparently he hadn't reconciled himself to the fact that a woman, traveling by herself, had him looking down the wrong end of his own .44.

"Well, what do you want?" the attendant asked.

"Who were those men who just left?" The young man

continued to look defiant. "I asked a question. Don't be rude," she said as she pulled back the hammer of the revolver.

"They, ah, they work for the railroad."

"What are their names, and what were they doing here?"

"Henderson and McLeish, and they was just shootin' the breeze," the man answered with no hesitation.

"What were they doing here?" Jessie asked again, a bit more insistent.

The attendant swallowed hard. "Uh, they put two fellows on the mornin' work train and were takin' their time about leavin'."

"All right, outside." She gestured with the gun. At first, the young man looked as if he were about to protest, but then he thought better of it. He led the way outside.

Jessie was going to gather some rope and tie the attendant up outside. Then she saw the boxcar sitting on the siding and ushered him to it.

"Inside," she ordered once they got in front of it. The young man climbed into it without comment, but he had a sour expression on his face. "Now, close the door." The door closed with a resounding thud. Jessie slipped the bolt. It seemed secure, but as an added measure, she called out loudly, "I'll be sitting out here enjoying some fresh air, and if I even see you peeking out I'm going to part your hair with this .44." She walked around the other side and made sure that door was also shut tightly. She didn't know if there was a trap in the roof, or if there was, if it was accessible from the inside. But she didn't really care. She didn't think the depot attendant had the nerve to chance getting shot, and she would be back for him in a very short time.

She returned to the shack. It was like a hundred other depots. There was one small room furnished with a cot, stove, a chair and a makeshift desk, and on the desk was the telegraph key. Jessie sat down in the chair and thought a moment. She picked up a pad and pencil and wrote out a short note and then did some rearranging of the letters.

To any one else the note was a jumble of letters. She reached for the telegraph and began sending. Once again, she was grateful to her father for insisting she learn Morse Code. And Alex Starbuck made sure his daughter not only learned the code, but could use it efficiently.

As she walked back to the boxcar, she wondered about the attendant's involvement with the cartel. When she first burst into the shack, she thought she saw a glimmer of recognition in his eyes. Did he know who she was and the fate that had been planned for her? That would explain his surprised look; no one walks away from a dynamited coach car. His move to his gun also substantiated her suspicions. But now she wasn't so certain of that. His surprise could be explained simply enough; it was a natural reaction, and the flash of recognition in his eye was probably due to his sizing up of the situation and not due to his knowing Jessica Starbuck. It was not unusual to have a sixth sense about danger, and it wouldn't have taken the attendant long to feel that he was in a dangerous situation. The pointed derringer was a dead giveaway. Also, his reaching for his gun was a natural reaction under the circumstances.

Fighting the cartel, Jessie remembered, produced an inherent sense of fear. It was often self-preserving. But Jessie had to fight the impulse to find a snake under every stone. It was quite possible that the drawing of his gun was not an admission of any guilt. Jessie would keep a close eye on him, but she was ready to give him the benefit of the doubt.

She slid open the door of the boxcar, and it came as no surprise that the attendant was right where she left him. "That wasn't so bad, was it?" she said as she gestured for him to jump out.

He rubbed his eyes as they adjusted to the bright daylight. "Now what?" he asked.

"Back into the shack." She still had the gun pointing at him. Until she was sure, there was no sense taking a chance.

Inside, she made him sit down at the desk. "I want you

to send this telegram," she said as she handed him a slip of paper.

"I don't know how to," the young man stammered.

Apparently the confinement in the boxcar had made him feisty, but Jessie was in no mood for games. "You'd better learn right quick!" she snapped. The attendant stared at her defiantly.

Brandishing the weapon, Jessie began to think out loud. "It's a pretty heavy gun, must have a lot of recoil." She chose her words carefully. "But then I reckon it would only take one shot." The young man's eyes went wide. Jessie continued, "At this range even a lady would have a hard time missing."

"I think I may be able to manage," he said with a gulp and then extended his hand to take the piece of paper.

"I certainly hope so," Jessie said as she suppressed her smile and handed him the message.

He read the note and then his eyes lit up. "You know Commodore Whiting?" he blurted incredulously.

Jessie nodded. "That's who the telegram is for, isn't it?"

"Well, why didn't you say so in the first place?"

"I didn't know it would matter," Jessie replied quite honestly.

"I never would have sassed you like that, ma'am, if I had known. I work for Commodore Whiting; in fact, he owns all this here."

Jessie couldn't hold back her laugh. "I know. I'm good friends with him, and I'm working for him, too." She lowered the gun and sat down on the edge of the desk. She no longer had any doubts about the young man's allegiance.

"I once met him in St. Paul," he said proudly. "He shook my hand and told me that, if I kept my eyes open and learned fast, one day I could own my own railroad just like him."

"I wouldn't be surprised. What's your name?"

"Sam. Sam Farley."

"Well, Sam, don't you think you should be getting that telegram off?"

"Yes, ma'am, right away." He turned to the telegraph key. Jessie could see the sheepish grin on his face as he added, "It was just a fib, what I said before. I can use this thing better'n most."

"I'm glad to hear it, Sam," Jessie said as she went over and sat down on the cot. As it was being sent, Jessie stretched out and relaxed. For the first time since arriving, Jessie felt in control. The pieces were finally fitting together.

After sending the telegram, Sam turned to Jessie. "Is Commodore Whiting really going to come out here? It must be important for the head of the railroad to come all the way out to the railhead."

"That's why I sent the message, Sam. It is important and I think he will come."

"Gosh!"

"Now, how about some lunch for your guest, Sam?" Jessie realized that she hadn't eaten since breakfast and now, with things looking up, was absolutely ravenous.

Sam fixed her a simple, satisfying meal of ham and beans. "If you ever get tired of workin' the rails, Sam, you can always come down to Texas and fix chow for my crew," she said good-humoredly.

"Texas? Is that where you're from?" Jessie nodded. "Maybe one day I'll do that," he added, "after I have a road of my own, of course."

Jessie smiled and stood up. "How do I get back to the railhead?"

"There's a handcar 'round back."

"Let's go," Jessie said eagerly. Sam hopped to his feet. They headed out the door.

A large canvas covered the metal workings of the hand-car, protecting them from the elements and keeping the parts from rusting. Sam threw back the covering and then gave Jessie a hand up. "All aboard the railhead express!" he shouted gaily.

They stood opposite each other and worked the lever

together. They were making good time when Jessie suddenly stopped and pulled the revolver from her waistband. "Before I forget, here," she handed Sam's gun back to him.

"Thanks," he said gratefully and shoved it into his waistband.

"You're standing a might bit taller now than you're packing your revolver again." There was some truth to her playful gibe.

"Thanks," Sam repeated.

Jessie resumed pumping the lever, but talked as she worked. "That your first gun, Sam?"

He shook his head. "I had an old Sharps, but that was just for hunting."

There was an unspoken subtlety there that Jessie disapproved of. The Sharps was a hunting rifle and, therefore, not as special as a six-shooter, which was for shooting men. That was part of the code of the West, and Jessie made no mention of it. She had grown up with it and would probably die with it, for there was no way of anything changing in the foreseeable future. "But this Remington is your first revolver?" she asked, although she knew the answer.

Sam nodded his head. "Yup."

"It's the Army model, isn't it?"

"That's right." Sam seemed impressed by her knowledge. "My dad swears by it."

Jessie smiled to herself. The Army model was liked, but was not suited to the fast draw. "It's an awfully heavy gun, Sam, and its long barrel makes it awkward for the fast draw."

"Yeah." Sam's interest was raised.

"That's about an eight-inch barrel you got there. That's a mighty long way to go to have to clear the holster. You should try the Navy model."

"Aw, but that's just a .36 caliber."

Again, Jessie smiled to herself and shook her head. There was always that fascination with size. "But it's a lighter gun with a shorter barrel. And who knows, with the Navy model things might have gone down differently back at the depot," she said with a wink.

"Maybe, but—"

"You don't like taking advice about guns from a woman, do you?"

"I didn't say that," he was quick to reply. But then he didn't deny it.

"Hand me your gun," Jessie said as she put out her hand. "And stop the car." Sam did as he was told. Jessie looked around for a suitable target and singled out a fallen pine about thirty yards from the track. She cocked the hammer and held the gun with both hands. "See that knot on the upper right," she said as she widened her stance.

Sam had just finished nodding when the gun exploded. It had a sharp recoil, but Jessie expected as much. The knot burst, after being hit dead center.

"Golly." Sam responded.

"With my Colt .38, I would have only needed one hand to steady the gun." Jessie didn't like showing off, but she wanted to make her point. "Later on, if you need a heavier caliber, you can try a Colt Peacemaker."

"I'll remember that," Sam said, and he probably would.

"But now let's get rolling again."

They both picked up the lever and were moving at a good clip when a thought struck Sam. "Jessie, I don't reckon there will be, but what if there's a westbound train runnin'?" There was genuine concern in his voice.

Jessie smiled. "We better pump fast—and hope."

Chapter 12

Ki had started out following the tracks, but soon realized that he would make better time by heading due west. The tracks also went west, but there were so many switchbacks along the route that Ki felt it would be wiser to follow a more direct path, even if it entailed going up and down a number of gulches and gullies. A less nimble man would have found it too exhausting and would have made better time following the flat, meandering right of way. But Ki scampered up and down the embankments without much difficulty. He was careful to keep a sharp eye out for the poisonous copperheads that were almost indistinguishable from the sandy rocks and pebbles. Furthermore, he found the climbing a welcome change from the monotony of following the well-laid tracks. Picking out the best path up or down a rocky slope kept his mind active.

When he set out, he sounded confident, but much of that was for Jessie's sake. He wanted to leave her with a sense of purpose and make her feel that they were closing the rope around the cartel's neck. Yet they had so damned little to go on. Schmitt had died too soon.

Ki hadn't lied to Jessie about letting the cartel agent come to him, but just how easy that would be remained to be seen. Sometimes, though, events took care of themselves.

Here in the West, the natural elements played as large a part in determining fate as the imposed structures of man. Ki chortled to himself. Throw in the cartel, and you add even more variables and unknowns. Thinking it over, he was almost amazed that they continued to triumph over the evil syndicate. Even the greatest general or samurai could make one mistake, and often that first mistake would be the last one. When the stakes were high, one slip would often be fatal.

Absorbed in his thoughts, Ki lost sight of the tracks. He thought about doubling back, but then decided against it. He wasn't sure exactly where Gilman's Crossing was, but felt if he continued due west he would eventually find it or come to a road that would lead to his ultimate destination, Basin City.

He followed a small stream up into the timbered hills and then turned to his left, to what he hoped was west, but with the sky still overcast, it was impossible to be absolutely sure. The wooded land offered a nice change of pace, however.

Cutting through the forested slopes, he would be entertained by the scurrying of small animals. Long-eared hares would hop out of his way, bushy-tailed squirrels would dart up trees, and mountain chipmunks would dive down into their holes seeking safety. Once he even passed a grazing mule deer. The golden young fawn, no doubt born that spring and not yet filled with the fear of man, stood her ground and continued to munch on small leaves and berries. Ki stopped and watched her and then slowly moved up on her, seeing how close he could come before she would bolt. He moved silently, but the amount of noise he made was irrelevant. The fawn could smell his presence as he stood upwind from her. But even now, as he moved closer to the animal, she did not take flight, but rather backed up with a slow indifference. The fawn went about her business, nonchalantly keeping her distance. Periodically her big brown eyes turned to study the approaching man. But Ki was not fooled. At the first sudden move, she would be gone, her white butt flashing through the woods.

For a moment Ki considered using this opportunity to practice the technique that he had used the other day on the wolf. The challenge of reaching out and touching the velvet soft nose of the fawn seemed almost too irresistible to pass up, but Ki dismissed it as a selfish act. Dealing with the wolf on its terms was one thing, but the one act of befriending the baby deer could prove to be the animal's undoing. If she were to associate the scent of other men with the gentleness of Ki, she would be easy prey for a hunter's bullet.

Just as Ki turned away from the deer, there was the loud crack of a rifle. The deer bolted. The sound came from the wrong direction to indicate a hunter. Off to his right, he heard the indistinct yells of a man in trouble. Ki turned and raced in that direction.

Over the rise, the timber opened into a small meadow. At the far end, Ki saw the reason for the gunshot and the yelling, and he stopped dead in his tracks. A large grizzly was clawing at the base of a tree. A few feet up, an old man clung precariously to a limb. He was high enough to avoid the sharp claws of the bear, but low enough to encourage the animal to swipe at him. However, it was probably only a matter of time before the frustrated bear would climb the tree. The man was well aware of this and was shouting every known obscenity in an effort to scare away the bear. Unfortunately, the shot Ki heard had wounded the bear in the shoulder. It was not a serious injury to the bear, but it angered the animal sufficiently so that the chance of its running off was now unlikely. On the ground lay a Springfield rifle, probably swatted down by the bear before another shot could be fired.

Ki's immediate reaction was to reach for a *shuriken*, though he doubted it would do any good. The throwing stars had a limited range. To be most effective they had to be thrown from a distance that would allow them a considerable speed. They could be thrown far, but their power at impact was greatly diminished if they covered too much ground. And right now Ki judged the distance to be too far. There was also the question of whether the tiny throwing star would have much effect on the large grizzly. From the back it was virtually impossible to hit the animal's jugular, and a hit anywhere else would be nothing more than an annoyance to the already infuriated beast. Ki figured the most vulnerable spots would be the bear's eyes or ears. But again, with the grizzly's back to him, neither target was in sight.

The bear seemed to be tiring of his futile attempts at bringing down his prey with a swipe of his paw, and it now looked like it was getting ready to climb the trunk of the tree. Ki was forced into taking any kind of direct action that might divert the bear's attention. If he could get the grizzly away from the tree long enough for the man to retrieve his rifle and if he were an accurate shooter . . . There were a lot of ifs, but something had to be done and done soon.

Ki took a deep breath, expanding his lungs to the fullest, and then quickly expelled the air in a loud shout. This yell would often accompany a strike in order to add increased power to the blow. The yell helped channel the energy of the breath into the force of the strike and, when done correctly, could produce an immensely powerful impact. By concentrating only on the abdominal muscles, all energy centered on expelling the breath up and through his vocal chords. The thundering cry that came out was more of a roar than a yell. The bear turned instantly. Ki was about to give another when the grizzly started to charge him. Apparently the animal took the yell as a cry of defiance and was quick to meet the challenge.

Ki stood his ground; there was no reason to run. If the

rifle wouldn't drop the beast, his only other chance lay in a well-placed *shuriken* or two. He watched as the angry grizzly rushed toward him. For an animal that weighed at least eight hundred pounds, it moved very fast. Looking into its fiery eyes, Ki could understand why an angered grizzly was so feared. For a brief instant, Ki wondered whether to be more careful of the sharp teeth or the powerful claws. Ki had a bad feeling that if it came down to a struggle with the beast it wouldn't really matter. He sincerely hoped it wouldn't come down to that. He could understand too why the grizzly bear was officially called *Ursus horribilis*. It was horrible!

Ki readied to throw the first *shuriken* when he heard a sharp crack. The bear let out a painful growl and slowed his lumbering mass. As it started to turn, there was another rifle crack, and the bear staggered, this time letting out a loud cry. Blood was pouring from a hole in its head. It took two more steps and then dropped.

Ki walked the few steps to the fallen mass of fur just as the marksman came bounding up.

"That yell came near to knockin' me clear out of my perch! But I'm mighty glad you showed up when you did." The man had a full head of long, straggly, white hair and a beard to match. His skin looked liked tanned leather and it was impossible to place his age. He looked old, but walked with a light step.

"And I'm glad you have a keen eye and a steady hand," Ki replied.

"I still got the eye I had as a boy. But when it goes, I reckon it's time to move on to greener pastures, if you get my drift." He turned to the bear and remarked, "My, but he was a mean one."

"I thought they didn't usually attack man," Ki said.

"Usually they don't. Unless, of course, it's a mother and her cubs. This beast ain't no lady." He bent down and lifted one of the grizzly's lips. "Well, that there explains it."

"What does?"

"She's an ol' soremouth."

"A soremouth?" Ki repeated, smiling.

"Sure, take a look at them back teeth." The trapper held up the lip again, and Ki could see a row of rotted teeth. "Rotted clear through to the nerve. Makes 'em terrible mean and I can't say I blame 'em. Once had a toothache that hurt like the dickens. Not even a bottle of my finest mash would do the trick. And these poor critters can't even take to the bottle."

Ki smiled at that. The man, not used to much company, continued to ramble on. "The greatest solace to man since women, the bottle is." He thought a minute and then added, "Or maybe the good Lord done give us the bottle after he realized what a problem women could be." He let out a hearty laugh. "Don't get me wrong, son, I love 'em. Enough of my jawin'. The way I see it, half this hide is yours." He pulled out a skinning knife and dropped down to his knees.

"Thanks, but you can have my share."

"You sure? Make a mighty nice coverin' when the snows hit." Ki shook his head. The man stood up and sheathed his knife. "In that case I'll skin it later. Right now, I'm passin' 'round the bottle. I'm shacked out not far from here."

"Are you a trapper?" Ki asked.

"A trapper, a prospector, a wolfer, a tracker," he replied with a smile and then extended his hand. "The name's Stone, but my friends call me Stoney."

Ki introduced himself, and they shook hands. A short walk later, they were sitting inside a wooden lean-to excavated into the base of a hill. The lodging was deceptive; outside it appeared small, but inside it was large and roomy and held all the comforts of home, including a few books that sat prominently on a wooden shelf.

Stoney offered drink, of which Ki took sparingly, and a hearty stew, of which Ki helped himself to seconds. "This is some of the best I've had," Ki said as he swallowed another mouthful.

"Should be, took me years to perfect." He leaned closer

and added in hush tones, "Don't try to wrangle the recipe from me, least not till I'm on my deathbed."

They talked more over lunch. Stoney remarked, "Came out to California in forty-nine and I've been movin' ever since. Now that the railroad's comin' through here, it looks like I'll be pickin' up again."

At the mention of the railroad, Ki realized that there was still work to do. "How do I get to Gilman's Crossing?" Ki asked.

"What you goin' there for? Ain't nothin' there but a water depot, a stable, and a two-bit cathouse."

"I'm really heading to Basin City and—"

"Well, why didn't you say so? There's a town that has everything a man could want."

"How far a walk is it?" Ki asked.

"Walk nothin'." Stoney slapped his thigh angrily. "The man done save my life and he won't even accept the hospitality of one of my burros."

"That's very nice of you, Stoney," Ki answered.

"Matter of fact, I'm short some sundries, too, and could do with a trip to town myself. If you don't mind the company . . ."

"Don't see how I could refuse," Ki said, smiling.

Ki was grateful for the company, but during the ride, Stoney managed to weasel from Ki his reason for going to town. Ki explained the situation to him, but left out pointed reference to or mention of the cartel. There were enough crooked outfits in operation that Stoney was able to grasp the picture without hearing about the international syndicate.

Stoney was quick to offer his assistance to Ki. "I don't have all that much love for the railroads. Given my druthers, I'd run 'em all off, but I reckon we're much better off with honest folk."

"I'm glad to hear you say it," Ki replied.

They rode in silence the remainder of the way. Stoney knew of a short cut that brought them to town before sundown, and as they approached, Ki could see why it was named Basin City. The town was tucked into a natural basin with good grazing and farmland stretched out around it. Basin City would inevitably grow as more of Oregon became settled, but right now it was hardly worthy of its designation as a city, even if, as Stoney promised, it offered everything a man would need or want.

Going down Main Street, Ki noticed why Stoney kept Basin City in such high esteem. There were any number of saloons, and many of the boarding houses at the end of the street had red lanterns hanging prominently over their doors. Most of the buildings were constructed of lumber and had the false façades that were so popular in frontier towns. The First Oregon Bank and the adjoining Oregon Central railroad office were the two exceptions, being constructed of thick brick. Obviously, the bank and the railroad shared the same vault, a practical and convenient situation, seeing as how they both handled large sums of money. Ki made a mental note to investigate any further connection between the bank and the cartel, and as they pulled up in front, Ki felt certain the association between the two went deeper than a shared vault. Jessie would have to make a new addition to her book. It worried Ki to see the spreading influence of the cartel so blatantly displayed. But that was all the more reason they had to continue their fight against the cartel.

The town merchants were beginning to close for the night, but there were still people in the railroad office. "Looks like they're open," Ki observed as he slid down from his saddle.

"I'll be across the street at the general store," Stoney said as he turned his burro.

"It looks like it might already be closed," Ki commented.

"Then I'll have to round up Jed from the back," Stoney answered with a chuckle. "He lives behind the store, and better now than when he's sittin' down to his evenin' meal. I won't be long."

Ki nodded and entered the railroad office. The oil lamps

had not yet been turned on, and it took a moment for his eyes to adjust to the gloom. The ticket vendor and cashier's cage were closed. Four tough men were sitting around one of the desks and playing cards.

"There ain't no trains till tomorrow. We're closed," one of them said gruffly without even looking up.

"I'm not interested in a train," Ki said flatly.

At that, one of the men looked up. "Hey, it's a Chinese."

"I'm looking for work."

"Well, we don't need a cook, but maybe you can wash my shirts." The others seemed to find that funny and broke into raucous laughter.

Ki said, "I heard you were looking for men who can handle themselves."

"Hey, Baker, I do believe this Chinaman is callin' you out."

Ki was not afraid of these drunken goons, but a brawl would not gain him any information. "No, I hire out and do what's supposed to be done, no questions asked."

His implication got through because Baker gave him a sideways look. "Who sent ya here?" he asked as he lay down his cards.

Ki thought about mentioning Spike or Schmitt and then decided against it. "That's not important. I'm here and willin'." One of the other men moved beside him. He was big and muscular, but Ki judged him to be slow and dim-witted.

"You look damn scrawny to be searchin' for a man's job," he said with a slurred tongue.

The man's motives were obvious—even without the encouragement of his friend who egged him on with a "Hey, Curly, bet you can take him out with one fist."

The tallest of the lot surprised Ki. "Watch out, Curly," he warned. "He may be one of those tong fellas from Frisco."

"Tong or no tong, Chuck, it ain't gonna matter much when I hit him with this."

Ki could see why Curly could be so confident. He had a punch that started from way down in his boots. Not many could stand up to such a wallop. But what gave the punch such power also telegraphed the move to a wise observer. Ki could see the shift in weight, the preliminary signal that the punch was on its way. By the time the blow was delivered, Ki had already stepped under the huge arm and given the off-balance Curly a shove from behind that sent him stumbling.

The huge man reeled on him, unsure of what happened, except that he had totally missed his intended victim. "Why, you measly . . ." he started to say as he threw another roundhouse.

But again Ki could spot it coming and sidestepped easily, this time though delivering a strong strike as Curly twisted around. The other toughs were beginning to stir. Once may have been luck, but twice . . . Curly was now enraged and threw caution to the wind. He lunged at Ki, both arms outstretched in an attempt to crush him in a bear hold. Ki sprung into a forward flying kick, hitting the surprised Curly smack in the face. He thought he could feel the slight give as front teeth gave way under his foot.

Curly brought his hands up to his bleeding mouth. "The son of a bitch knocked my teeth out," he cried as he spat blood and broken teeth.

Baker had seen enough. "Pull down those shades," he ordered the others. He lit the oil lamp that sat on the corner of the desk. As the light flared, they all got a better look at Curly's battered and bleeding face. Ki heard an astonished gasp from one of the men.

"Looks like we got some fun here, boys," Baker said as he stood up. They fanned out to surround Ki. "We're gonna teach the Chinaman here a lesson in manners he ain't gonna forget soon," he said threateningly.

As long as nobody pulled a gun, and he didn't think that was likely, Ki was not too worried. As a group, they were confident enough to feel that they could take him in a brawl, and pulling a gun on him would cheapen their victory, if not actually embarrass them. None of them would be too eager to admit that someone had to pull a gun to subdue one Chinaman.

Ki circled slowly, keeping an eye on each one. He also suspected that at least for a while they would come at him one at a time. It would take a few cracked ribs and broken bones before they would realize that their only hope lay in rushing him at once. But, of course, by then it would be too late.

Ki kept his eyes moving from one man to the next and paid little attention to their taunts and verbal threats. For all their talk, they were slow to act.

"I think he's gonna tire himself out with all that neck twisting he's doing," Baker said with a smirk.

"I say we get him before he gets too tired and dizzy to remember anything," Chuck said, though he took no action himself.

Ki was starting to tire, more from the monotony of the situation than from lack of energy. He was contemplating becoming the aggressor—when the door opened.

"Nobody was home, so—" Stoney began to say, but then stopped suddenly as he grasped the situation Ki was in. From underneath his jacket, he pulled out a .45. "All you gents back off against the wall," he ordered curtly.

"We ain't got no beef with you, old man," Baker told him."

Stoney cocked the hammer with his thumb. "You ain't gonna have a beef with nobody if you don't do as I say."

"Don't be foolish, old man. You might get yourself hurt," Baker said defiantly, though he did take a step back.

"I'm a man of few words, fellas. Y'all seem like a bunch of right nice folks so maybe I'll give y'all a little learnin' in gunsmithin'," Stoney said amiably.

Stoney may have been calm, but Ki was now even more alert. When the fight was hand to hand, Ki wasn't too worried. But now that Stoney pulled a gun, it was an open challenge. If there were one hotheaded fast draw among them, the lead would be flying soon. Stoney might be able to get one or two, but there were four of them, and those weren't good odds. Ki slipped his hand into his vest and took hold of a *shuriken*.

Stoney seemed to be reading his mind. "This here's not your ordinary .44. It'll fire six rounds before your Colt'll get off three. See, they squeeze .45 caliber shells in the same size cylinder, so the bullets are all that much closer to each other."

Ki could see them eyeing each other nervously. Ki slipped his hand out of his pocket. There was no reason to be sly. The faster he could let loose the throwing stars the better.

"And if any of you are curious as to just what one more caliber'll do to a hole in your chest, just make a move for your gun."

Ki could feel the tension in the air. Suddenly he saw Baker's arm move ever so slightly. The *shuriken* sped through the air. The blade dug itself into his forearm; there was a loud explosion. Smoke was drifting out of the six-shooter's barrel.

No one else had moved. Baker stood there in shock. "I've been stuck and shot, stuck and shot," he kept muttering. Blood was trickling down from where the *shuriken* was embedded in his arm, but the blood was pouring even more profusely from the tip on one of his fingers. Or to be more precise, from where the tip used to be.

"Damn! His trigger finger's blown off!" Chuck exclaimed.

"I was hoping it wouldn't come to this." Stoney's friendly tone was gone. "Now off with your guns and toss them through the window—one at a time." There was no hesitation. "His, too," Stoney said, gesturing to Baker, who was clutching his bleeding hand, still in shock.

Chuck went over and removed his boss's gun and then tossed it through the window. Only then did Baker realize the extent of his wound.

"My blasted trigger finger's gone; how am I gonna shoot, you old bastard?" Baker howled.

"I think your shootin' days are over, pardner," Stoney replied.

"You old bastard, you!" Baker repeated.

"I thought you might be showin' a bit more appreciation." The amiable tone returned to Stoney's voice. "Now, maybe you'll live to die of old age."

"Take it easy, Baker," Chuck said as he helped him into a chair.

"You boys sit tight and continue your card game, and I'll send the doctor over shortly. Ready, Ki?" With that, Stoney twirled the revolver neatly around his finger and then put the gun back into his waistband.

Out on the street, Stoney turned to his friend. "I was a little worried about you, Ki, but after I saw that tiny blade of yours, I reckon you can take care of yourself."

"I was concerned about you, too," Ki said with a smile, "but I see I had no reason to be. I didn't even know you were carrying a gun."

"I pack it when I come to town. Never know what I'll run into."

"And was that true about the gun?" Ki asked almost childishly.

"Just a little technical whoey to dazzle the opposition."

Ki thought it over. "Then if they all had drawn on you, they'd have had a good chance," he remarked a few steps later.

"They had no chance at all," Stoney said flatly. Ki detected a trace of sorrow in his words. A few steps later Stoney smiled and said almost jokingly, "I wasn't always an old trapper."

★

Chapter 13

"Sam, I want you to go right to the mess tent and stay there. Tell Pops you're a friend of mine. He'll look after you," Jessie instructed the young telegrapher as the small handcar turned onto the railhead siding.

"You sure you won't need my help?" Sam asked. He was well aware of the sabotage that had been plaguing the railroad, but had never suspected that the men that stopped in on him regularly were probably the culprits. Once Jessie explained the situation, he was eager to help rout the saboteurs from their lair.

"The best thing for you to do is just stay out of sight and trouble till I call for you."

"Whatever you say, Jessie."

"Oh, Sam, may I borrow your gun for a spell?"

Jessie wondered why the usually bustling camp seemed so quiet. Even at dinner time, men would always be milling around, smoking or playing cards. When she turned the corner at the lumberyard, she had the answer.

All the workers were gathered at the head of the tracks, and standing on the coal tender addressing them was Spike McCaully. Jessie did not like the look of it. Any gathering of the men was generally not good news, but if Spike were responsible for it, it could only spell trouble.

She started walking through the crowd when she spotted Pops standing at the edge of the gathering. "What's this all about, Pops?" she asked as she came up beside him.

"Why, Jessie," he said with surprise, "I thought you were on your way to take care of business."

"I changed my plans, and I think it's a good thing too!" she said as she looked around.

"They attacked the track layers today."

"Who?" Jessie asked quickly and then realized what the answer would be.

"The same stinkin' varmints who've been settin' fires and blowin' up our supplies."

"Anyone hurt?"

"Brunner took a slug in the leg, but he'll be okay."

"How did it happen?"

"Ain't much to tell, Jessie. Three men came ridin' out of the woods shootin'. Before the dust settled, they were gone, and Brunner was lyin' in the dirt bleedin'. We're lucky no one else got hurt. Shook the men up real bad though."

"That's exactly what it was supposed to do, Pops. And how'd this meeting start?"

"Don't rightly know," Pops said as he scratched his head. "Just seemed to happen, that's all."

"Does Gil know about this?"

"Spike sent someone out to fetch him." Jessie didn't seem pleased with that, and as soon as Pops said it, he realized why. "He could be in cahoots with 'em."

Jessie didn't know if he meant Spike or the messenger, but it didn't matter either way. She nodded her head and thought a moment. "Is there someone you trust whom we can send out now just in case Gil never gets the first message?"

"I reckon there is, but . . ." His hesitation was natural. At this point there was no one who could be absolutely trusted.

Suddenly the answer came to Jessie. "Pops, there's a friend of mine waiting in the mess tent. If you saddle him up a horse and give him directions . . ."

"I get the drift. I'm on my way." Pops was already heading for the tent.

Jessie rushed after him. "Oh, and tell him when he gets back I'll have a Navy model for him."

Pops looked confused. "A what?" he said as he scratched his gray whiskers.

"He'll know what I mean," Jessie said with a smile. "More important, he'll know that it's me doing the asking and that there's not some trickery afoot."

Pops nodded and hurried off. During her conversation with him, she was able to overhear enough of Spike and the crowd to get the general idea, but now she gave the gathering her full attention.

"Now, I ain't saying we should quit—" Spike said from atop the tender.

"Well, just what are you saying, Spike?" came the call from somewhere within the crowd.

"All I'm saying is that there ain't enough money to make me throw my life away!"

That got a stir from the men. "Y'ain't turnin' yella on us, are you, Spike?" someone else shouted. Nervous laughter passed through the crowd.

"Now, that ain't even a question as I see it." Many of the men laughed easily at that, and Spike continued, "We all knew the risks when we signed on, but now the stakes are just gettin' a little too high for my blood."

This all seemed very reminiscent of the meeting the men had a few nights ago, Jessie thought to herself, but then Gil was there to pull the workers back together. And until now she had not realized how well liked Spike was among the men.

"I reckon those of us who were gonna quit have already hit the rails," one of the workers stated. There was a lot of agreement with that.

"We're here to do the job!" exclaimed another.

Jessie was glad there was still a strong positive attitude among many of the workers. Those feelings were summed up best by one man who said, "I think many of us are here 'cause we don't cotton much to the idea of a bunch of thugs runnin' us off." Supportive cheers broke out among the crowd, and Jessie hoped that maybe the workers had rallied themselves and nipped the problem in the bud.

"We all agree on that, Hopkins," Spike answered. "We're here to finish this road. But we ain't doin' anybody any good if we go out and get shot up." Spike waited a moment for his words to sink in and then continued. "Dead men don't lay a good track!" Even Jessie realized the truth in his words. Sentiment was swinging back to Spike, and he pressed his advantage. "Like I said, I ain't sayin' we tuck in our tails and run. I just say we wait it out. Seems to me these men doin' the shootin ain't got no beef with us. The score they're out to settle is with the Wood River. Now, I say let the bosses settle their differences without puttin' us in the middle!"

There was a lot of agreement on that. The railroad executives, or brass collars as they were often called, were almost universally disliked by the railroad workers who would do the work, take the risks, and then get none of the credit. It wasn't so much the financial exploitation; they knew the wages when they signed on and were probably hard pressed to do any better even in another line of work. It was more the lack of respect. Many brass collars really did feel that the workers were an expendable commodity like coal or lumber. After they were used up, more could always be purchased or hired as the case might be.

"Ain't our job tough enough without gettin' shot at?" Spike asked the agitated crowd.

"Damn straight it is!" came the reply from more than one worker.

"I say we keep our heads in the tents and our asses in one piece till we can get back to building this road without being preyed upon."

"We're with ya, Spike," was the first response, and it was followed quickly by other endorsements.

The time to act was now. Jessie wasn't sure what to do, but she knew if she didn't act now, the men would follow Spike's lead and a striking crew was the last thing she wanted. She began to walk hurriedly through the crowd, geting her share of curious looks as she headed to the tender.

Spike noticed her a few yards from the tender. The expressions on his face ranged from surprise to anger and spoke volumes. Even though he instigated the men to strike, Jessie couldn't be sure of Spike's involvement with the cartel. Industry was forever turning out a few malcontents, and Spike's actions need not be the doings of the cartel. In fact, they were similar to the gripings of many an embittered worker—men who had given their best years to an industry and gotten little back in return; men who were ambitious but also lazy; men who wanted more but lacked either the courage, nerve, or simple gumption to pull themselves up by their bootstraps. Jessie had seen it on the ranges of Texas. Many an enterprising cowboy would slowly pack away his savings till he could buy a small spread of his own. And if the methods were not always honest (many a respectable rancher started his herd with a few rustled cattle), there were opportunities for those who dared. Yet many a haggard cowpoke would sit around the bunkhouse complaining about this or that, always pointing to the ranchers as the cause of his own failures. Men who weren't willing to work hard for what they wanted had to have a scapegoat. They would never place the blame where it belonged, on themselves. Instead, they found fault with their employers.

Jessie didn't know the railroad business that well, but

she did know that here, too, were men who started at the bottom and pulled themselves up.

It was quite possible that Spike McCaully was guilty of nothing more than spite, bitterness, and failed ambition. Then Jessie saw that look on his face. Suddenly she realized that his surprise at seeing her stemmed from his belief that by now she would be lying dead in the wreckage of a dynamited coach car. His anger was at having his plans foiled again.

If looks could kill, Jessie would now be lying face down in the dust, and even as she climbed atop the tender, she realized the distinct possibility that Spike in his seething fury would gun her down in cold blood. Her fears were soothed when she saw that Spike was not packing a gun. Without a word, Spike waved to the workers and jumped down from the tender.

Jessie steadied her footing on the pile of coal and looked out at the assembly of workers. She told herself this was no different from talking to her hands from the bunkhouse porch. She remembered the rapport Gil had with the men and, as she began to speak, hoped she could establish a similar relationship with them.

"I wish Gil were here to talk to you all," she started out saying, "but he's out working to make this road a reality. He's out surveying a trestle that he expects you men to build and lay tracks on."

"You can't lay tracks across a trestle that keeps gettin' blown up," a voice called out from the crowd.

"You've managed to come this far," Jessie replied.

"Dead men don't build good trestles," yelled the next heckler.

Jessie ignored the comment and the accompanying snickers, but wondered whether the heckler was a cartel agent or an honest, but defeated, man. "I don't think there are enough thugs to stop the course of progress, and every mile of track we lay is progress."

"And every man who gets shot holds up that progress,"

a sincere voice from the crowd stated.

Jessie realized she couldn't skirt the issue any longer. "There's a lot of truth to that, but I don't think that's the whole story." Jessie hoped she didn't ride herself into a box canyon. She swallowed and continued. "I don't think there's a man here who's afraid of a fight."

"That's right," came the first encouraging cry.

"But you've gotten to feeling that this is a one-way battle—that all you can do is stand by helpless and watch as bridges get burned or supplies are blown up."

"That's what's been happenin' all right."

"Well, I'm tired of watching all your hard labor going up in a puff of smoke," Jessie said angrily. "I think it's time we stopped letting it happen."

There were mixed emotions as she said that, ranging from the sarcastic "We'll just stop it, easy as a preacher on a Sunday ride" to the enthusiastic "The time to stop it is long overdue." But most of the reaction could be summed up in one brief question—How?

"No rider is going to come charging out of the woods when there are men watching with shotguns." That got them stirring. "And no one's going to sneak up on a supply hut when there are men posted who will shoot first and ask questions later."

"Those are mighty big words, lady," someone called out.

"And we're already short of men," chimed another.

"Trail drives are often short of men, but you work and sleep in shifts," she began. "I think it's a good deal better to have some men working and some men riding shotgun than to have a full crew looking like a flock of grazing sheep waiting for the coyote to strike. At first we'll make slower progress, but there won't be any more so-called accidents, and in the end we'll be moving at a better clip."

"Don't seem fair, though, that we should have to do that."

"No, it isn't, but tell that to the men who shot up Brunner," Jessie said hotly.

"They's paying us to lay tracks, not guard 'em," the same man shouted.

Jessie sought out the speaker from the crowd and made a mental note to remember his face. She was certain this one was working for the cartel. "They're paying you to get from here to the Pacific," she snapped.

"They're payin' us, but they don't give a hoot what happens to us," the same one responded.

"Most of you have worked on other roads, so you know it's true when I say that Commodore Whiting cares about you all."

"That's true. He even shook my hand," boasted one of the workers.

Jessie could barely suppress her smile. "You're not just track layers, or tie men, or rock crushers; you're a part of this railroad."

"I don't wanna be a part that's buried along the right of way," shouted another worker. Jessie quickly identified him. Now that things were moving, the cartel men were forced to come out in the open and voice their objections.

"The Wood River line has always been one of the safest railroads to work. And again that's because Commodore Whiting doesn't want to take needless chances with your lives. How many other railroads are running air brakes?" she asked.

"Yeah, but we're still out here takin' the risks, while the fat cats sit at home."

That made three cartel agents, and Jessie was ecstatic. Not because she was slowly singling them out, but because they couldn't have played into her hands better. "You're wrong about that, friend," she said confidently. "At this very moment, Commodore Whiting is riding the rails out here." A murmur rippled through the men. "He's coming to take charge of everything personally. And I say, why hold up work till he gets here? Let's show him we're every bit as good as he thinks we are."

"He's always been square with us," one man said.

"If *the* brass collar is gonna be standin' up long side us, I'll be damned if I'm gonna be sittin' on my butt." That brought laughs and cheers.

Jessie decided this was the time to pull the ace out of the hole. "Let's show Commodore Whiting we're worth that extra half dollar!"

At first there was bewilderment; then as the words sunk in and the awareness of the raise hit, the men eased into jubilant smiles. "That a guarantee?" someone shouted above the other happy voices.

"That's a promise!" Jessie said with a smile. It was time to wrap things up. "I say it's time we take a vote. And let it be the honest man who has nothin' to hide and nothin' to fear who votes to stay on and build clear through to the Pacific!" She caught her breath. "All those in favor, say aye," she bellowed.

Hands shot up, and voices cried out in unison. Only a handful of men kept their arms down and their mouths shut. But then one by one, for fear of censure, they raised their hands and joined the now unanimous vote.

Jessie climbed down from the tender. The immediate problem was taken care of, but a more sinister danger still existed: Spike McCaully. There was no longer any doubt about Spike's association with the cartel. He was, if not the top honcho, then at least the top cartel agent in the camp. And now that the men were solidly behind her, Spike would be forced to take the bull by the horns. Backed into a corner as he was, he would certainly make one last effort to get control of or totally ruin the camp. Jessie didn't want to second-guess him; she wanted to stop him. Whatever he planned would be desperate and deadly. She knew she couldn't give him the time or the freedom to act.

She walked directly to Spike's tent, threw open the flap, and stormed in. Her gun was drawn and ready.

Spike sat at a small rickety table in the back corner. At the sound he looked up, surprised.

"It would give me all too much pleasure to have you

reach for your gun," Jessie said calmly. Slowly Spike placed both his hands on the table. "But the federal marshal may have some questions he wants to ask you," Jessie added with a trace of disappointment.

Spike looked dumbfounded. "A man speaks his mind, and you call in a marshal. I got a right to voice my opinion."

"One man already voiced his opinion, and that's why the marshal is on his way."

A look of concern crossed Spike's face, but he tried to hide it. "There ain't nothing illegal about organizin' a strike," he said evenly.

"No, there isn't," she agreed.

"Then I'm getting up and walkin' straight out of here." Spike slowly got to his feet.

"If you make the door, it'll be with a large hole in your gut," Jessie informed him.

Spike sat back down.

"I'm not dumb, Spike. You were under suspicion for a while, but we had no hard evidence on you." Spike squirmed uncomfortably in his seat. "Until now," Jessie added.

"You got nothin' on me 'cause I didn't do a thing." Spike spat out the words.

"That's not what Schmitt says." Jessie noticed the color drain from Spike's face. "Schmitt spilled the beans to save his hide. Right now I suspect he's sitting safely behind bars, and Ki and the marshal are heading this way."

"You can't keep me prisoner. Any of the men walk in and they'll think you've gone loco."

Jessie almost enjoyed watching Spike try to weasel out of this, but she had also wondered what others would think if they saw her. She also worried about the other cartel men who were still on the loose about camp. For the first time she noticed that Spike seemed edgy, his eyes darting nervously. Was he waiting for one of his accomplices to stick his head into the tent? She moved to the cot and sat down with her back against the canvas wall. A dirty shirt was lying next to her. She picked it up and placed it over her gun. A casual observer would notice only that Jessie had her hands in her lap and they were covered by a shirt. But the barrel of the gun remained trained on its target.

"If anyone comes in, we're having a friendly chat. I wouldn't want to put an unnecessary hole in this shirt," Jessie said dryly.

"You won't get away with this."

There was a tone of defiance in his voice that Jessie didn't like. Did he have something planned that would not be affected by his detention? She decided to press her advantage. "You're on the wrong side of this .44 to be acting cocky. No matter what happens out there, I still have you on the business end of this Remington." For a brief moment Spike once again looked like a hog-tied bull. "It's time to lay down your cards, Spike. If there's anything planned, call it off. Start talking and it'll go easier on you."

"I'll do my talking to the marshal." Spike spat on the floor. "If he gets here," he added.

Jessie smiled to herself. Once again at ease, Jessie decided to ask Spike something that had been nagging at her from the start. "Why did you throw in with the cartel, Spike?" she asked sincerely. "You've been working for the railroads your whole life. Many a man would be pleased to be construction foreman."

"Yeah, I've been workin' my whole life on the roads, and I want more than to die in a dusty tent with calluses on my hands and holes in my boots."

Just then they heard footsteps behind the tent. Both Jessie and Spike focused attention on the sound. "See who that is," Jessie instructed softly, her eyes keenly watching her target.

Spike returned her stare and, without turning away, called out. "Otto, that you?" There was a muffled reply. Then Spike broke out into a grin. "Bring her in, Otto," he said ominously.

The rear tent flap was pulled back and Otto, pushing Cynthia Johnson ahead of him, stepped into the tent. Cynthia was bound securely and gagged with a bandanna. Her eyes were wide with terror. The barrel of a sawed-off shotgun pressed firmly into her soft white throat.

Spike let out an ugly laugh. Jessie lowered her gun.

★

Chapter 14

"Was she any trouble?" Spike asked Otto.

"The she-devil bit my hand while I was keeping her mouth shut." He held up his hand to show the bloody marks. As he spoke, Jessie detected the slight trace of a Prussian accent.

"Is that what took so long?" Spike continued.

"I was trying to have a little fun; I didn't think you'd mind," Otto replied sheepishly.

Cynthia's dress was indeed torn, exposing her frilly slip. In the few days that Jessie had known Cynthia, this was the second time her dress had been ripped in that fashion. It was no time for humor, but Jessie realized with a silent chuckle that among certain company a full, well-rounded bosom took an awful toll on a lady's wardrobe.

Spike gave Cynthia a thorough visual inspection. "How was it?" he asked with a leer.

"I told you, she bit my hand!" Otto said dejectedly.

"Don't fret, Otto; you'll get your chance." The implications were obvious enough, but Spike's voice had an added edge that made Cynthia's eyes flicker with fear.

"What are we gonna do with her?" Otto gestured to Jessie.

Spike let out a hearty laugh. "More of the same, and I'll see to it personally."

"That's good." Otto was virtually drooling at the thought.

"But for now tie her up." Spike walked to the cot and, reaching underneath it, pulled out some rope and a gunbelt. He threw the rope to Otto and then pulled a Colt .44 from its holster. "It would also give me great pleasure to plug you full of holes," he said as he leveled the gun on Jessie, "but first there are some holes of your own I'm gonna plug real good." He gave another ugly laugh. "I like my meat squirmin' and scratchin'!"

Jessie said nothing for fear that any remark would only encourage him more. She needed time to figure a way out and didn't want to provoke the hotheaded, cocky foreman.

Otto came over and forced her hands together behind her back. She let out a little cry of pain. "Ah, this is a delicate one," Otto exclaimed meanly. Jessie was not in pain, but she wanted to distract Otto while she twisted her wrists around slightly. They were now almost perpendicular to each other and would not be tied as tightly together as they would have been had her wrists lay flat together. She cried out again. "It's too tight. You're cutting off my circulation," she protested.

Smiling, Otto tugged a bit harder on the rope and then tied the knot. Jessie's complaint had fooled Otto into believing the rope was tighter than it really was, so even with the extra tug, Jessie felt there would be enough slack to wriggle free. Otto examined the knot; the rope was digging into her flesh. "You won't be going anywhere," he exclaimed, "but to be on the safe side . . ." He grabbed Cynthia and threw her down on the cot next to Jessie. "Get your legs up," he ordered and then began to tie Jessie's and Cynthia's ankles together.

For a moment, Jessie feared he would discover the derringer that was holstered in her boot, but Otto never reached far enough up her calf to feel the tiny gun. As she watched Otto tie their ankles, she couldn't help thinking it was a lot of work for nothing. If she managed to get her hands free, the ropes around their legs would come off easily, no matter how well they were tied. And if their hands remained tied, it was unlikely they would go running off. She suspected that Spike would not let his two prize possessions lie there unguarded, no matter how well Otto tied the ropes.

The next indignity came when Otto removed the soiled and sweaty bandanna from around his neck and used it to gag Jessie.

"Good, now go round up the rest of the boys," Spike instructed Otto when he had finished tying the women. He then picked up the blanket from the foot of the cot and threw it over Jessie and Cynthia. Jessie couldn't decide if the blanket was to keep the other cartel members from knowing Spike held them hostage or to keep Jessie from seeing who the other cartel agents were. Probably some of both.

After a few moments, Jessie could hear the tent flap open repeatedly, and by counting the scuffling of boots, Jessie figured four men had entered, but Jessie wasn't sure whether or not that included Otto.

"Wednesday mornin' we're all gonna meet up at the depot. Get the word around to the others. Tomorrow me and Otto are headin' off to Basin City," Spike announced.

"What about the camp?" one of the others asked. Under the blanket Jessie listened intently. She recognized the speaker as one of the troublemakers from the meeting.

"We're pullin' out."

"Spike, you ain't lettin' that petticoat get the better of us are you?" Jessie wondered if he would expose them now or keep them secret.

"In two days this camp won't mean nothin'," Spike replied. He didn't make any mention of the two women. "After one more raid, they'll be throwing down their picks and shovels," Spike added.

"Yeah, we ain't 'fraid of a few men with guns. An if we strike fast, they won't even have their watches organized," a second voice added, referring to the guards Jessie suggested they begin to post. Again Jessie recognized the speaker as one of the hecklers in the crowd.

"We're not runnin' scared. We got bigger fish to fry," Spike stated proudly. "In two days this camp will be shut down, and the railroad will be finished. Henderson knows the plan. Now get goin'."

Jessie heard men leave; then Otto spoke up. "What about them?" he asked excitedly.

"We'll save them for Fannie's cat house, where we can do them right," Spike replied. From the tone in his voice, Otto had other ideas. "It's too risky here, Otto," Spike explained. Otto began to voice his objections when Spike cut him off. "You'll wait till we get to Basin City," he said sharply. Then he softened his tone and said, "And besides, at Fannie's they can scream their fool heads off and no one will care."

"That is good," Otto said agreeably.

Jessie could feel Cynthia tremble ever so slightly.

"Make yourself comfortable, Otto. I want you to keep an eye on them."

"All night?"

"Yeah. You can sleep on the way to Basin City," Spike said and then left the tent.

Jessie heard Otto pull up a chair and, with a heavy sigh, lower himself into it. Jessie listened closely to the man's breathing. As the night progressed, she hoped that Otto would feel confident enough and tired enough to doze. It seemed like an endlessly long time before his breathing slowed and became heavy. Still, Jessie wasn't convinced he was asleep. Then there was a short snore and she was certain.

The first thing Jessie did was press her wrists flat together. That position caused some slack in the rope, enough, she hoped, to enable her to squirm free. She began to wriggle her wrists, little by little, slipping the rope lower down her wrists. It was slow work, and for a moment Jessie thought she should have begun to slip free hours ago. But she wanted to make sure Otto was fast asleep. Even the slightest movement under the blanket might have stirred his curiosity, and Jessie didn't want to be discovered with half-untied ropes.

Jessie continued at a frustrating pace, sometimes just wanting to scream and thrash about. But each wiggle brought progress, even if it was only the width of a hair. Jessie felt Cynthia stir and begin to wiggle up against her. They were lying on their sides, back to back. Apparently, Cynthia realized what Jessie was trying to do and was now trying to get her hands in a position where she could help. It took a little more wriggling, but soon Jessie could feel Cynthia's hands. Jessie felt for the knot that held Cynthia, but her fingers were crammed too close together to permit her any movement, and without use of her thumbs, it was impossible to get any leverage against the tight knot. Jessie could feel Cynthia trying the same thing with no better results.

Jessie resumed her slow wiggling against her bonds, but this time she felt Cynthia using the tips of her fingers to help slide the rope down. Working in unison, Jessie twisting and Cynthia pushing, they soon freed Jessie's thumb. And with one thumb loose, there was enough slack to get the other one loose. A moment later, Jessie had both hands free. She quickly got to work untying Cynthia.

They lay there for another moment, just to make sure Otto was still asleep. When Jessie heard nothing but deep breathing and an occasional snore, she sat up quickly and pulled the derringer from her boot. While she kept it trained on their sleeping guard, Cynthia removed their gags and untied their feet.

Soundlessly they got up. It must have been earlier than Jessie thought because the oil lamp was still burning. Otto was fast asleep, his rifle resting peacefully in his lap. Jessie walked to the table and picked up her revolver. Cynthia went over to the tent flap.

Suddenly, Jessie heard someone stumble and give out a short cry. She reeled and quickly shoved the barrel of the gun against Otto's forehead. With her other hand, she knocked away his rifle. Otto woke quickly and started to get up when he realized the pressure against his head was the barrel of a .44. Confused, he sat back down and tried to make sense of things.

Jessie, too, was trying to figure out what had happened. But then Cynthia walked back into the tent with Spike's gun pressed against her head. It looked like a classic Mexican stand-off: Jessie's gun on Otto and Spike's gun digging into Cynthia's temple. Jessie had a feeling it wouldn't last and she would wind up the loser. Otto was expendable to Spike, whereas Jessie did not want to see Cynthia get hurt, and they both knew it. She lowered her gun.

"You idiot!" Spike snapped at Otto. "It's a good thing I was sleeping right outside. If she hadn't tripped on me, they would have gotten away."

What had happened became clear to Jessie. Spike had been sleeping right outside the tent. On clear nights that was not unusual; the air was thick and hardly circulated inside the tents, and if Spike dragged a cot from another tent, he would have raised no suspicions. As Cynthia had stepped out of the tent, her eyes had not adjusted to the darkness, so she had gone sprawling over Spike's cot. That explained the little cry. The rest was obvious.

"Take your gun," Spike said with disgust, "and go hitch up the wagon." Otto did as he was told, and Spike turned his attention to Jessie. "I think we can dispense with the gags. One sound and I'll blow her brains out the other side of her head. I'll tell anyone who wants to know that I heard some rustlin' round the tent and took a shot. With all the sabotage goin' 'round, no one'll give it a second thought."

Jessie knew he was right and nodded agreement. She

was glad she slipped her derringer back in her boot after she had picked up the heavier gun. It might prove life-saving later.

When they heard the wagon roll around out front, Spike picked up the rope and pointed to the flap. "The first sound and she's dead," Spike cautioned as he began to back out of the tent.

"Spike, wait." Jessie pleaded in a low whisper. She had to say something now before they got outside. Spike, holding Cynthia firmly, stepped back into the tent. "Let her go. You don't need her."

"She's our insurance policy," Spike replied.

"She's nothing to you and you have me. There's no good reason to drag her along," Jessie continued to plead.

"I can think of two good reasons," Spike said as he leered at her breasts.

Jessie ignored that and continued trying to reason with him. "Two of us can only be added trouble. You'll have to watch us constantly. You've seen what almost happened. Let her go and I'll give my word that I'll behave."

Spike seemed to like the idea of Jessie keeping in line. "You can be a heap of trouble," he said to himself.

"I'll sit up front with you, and when we ride into town, you can act as if I'm your girl."

"But what about her?"

"She doesn't know anything. And she'll give you her word not to say anything. There's no evidence against you 'cept for us two. If you let her go, she won't talk, and I'll . . ." There was no reason to finish the statement.

Spike was thinking it over. "You want me to let her go. What's in it for me?"

Jessie smiled to herself. The trait that often induced men to work for the cartel was also their weakness: greed. There was always a price at which men like Spike could be bought. "As you might know, I'm a woman of some wealth. When we get to town, I can wire for money—more money than you'll get from the cartel."

"Is that before or after the night at Fannie's?" Spike asked.

"If I said before, would we have a deal?"

"I kinda had my heart set on it . . ." There was no gentleness in his words.

"Then after," Jessie answered without hesitation. There was another trait besides greed that marked a cartel agent: dishonesty. Jessie knew that Spike's word meant little. He would do as he pleased. Jessie hoped, though, that she could make an attractive enough offer to save Cynthia.

"It's still too risky to leave her here."

"Then at the water depot. The attendant's gone. Lock her in the shack; by the time anyone discovers her, it'll be too late."

"I'll ponder it on the way." His tone made it very clear the negotiations were over. "What I said's still true. Not a sound," he warned as he ushered the women outside.

It was a moonless night, and the darkness was almost absolute. Jessie could understand how Cynthia had tripped; she probably would have done the same herself. Even she couldn't see the wagon until they were right on top of it. Spike pushed them into the wagon and threw the rope to Otto. "Tie 'em back to back and don't worry about their hands. I'll be back here watchin' 'em just in case."

As Otto climbed into the wagon, a thought crossed his mind. "What about Gil?"

"He shouldn't be any the wiser," Spike answered.

"Yeah, but if he gets wind of—"

Spike cut him off. "For his sake I hope he steers clear. He wouldn't want to see what I'm going to do to these two young fillies."

Jessie turned quickly. Her voice was low, but her words were sharp. "I told you, it'll be worth your while to let her go."

Even in the dark, Jessie could see Spike's ugly smile as he leaned close. "Otto wouldn't like that very much, would he? Now let's move," he said, turning to his henchman.

Otto climbed into the seat and took hold of the reins. There was a little jerk that sent Jessie and Cynthia tumbling to their sides and then the wagon vanished into the night.

★

Chapter 15

Gil came charging into the camp a little before sunrise. He had been riding through the night to arrive in camp as dawn broke. Originally he hadn't intended to come at all.

When Sam first appeared at the surveying camp, Gil was immediately suspicious. His urgent message could have been another ruse to divert Gil and further delay the building of the trestle. Gil had even turned in for the night before he began having second thoughts. If there really were trouble brewing at the railhead, his absence from there would do more harm to the railroad than his absence from the trestle site. The trestle could be delayed a day or two, but if the men were to strike, it would prove disastrous. More important, what if Jessie needed him?

He had pulled himself from his bedroll and went to question the young telegrapher. He grilled the boy, hoping to catch him in some slip, but Sam kept to his original story. He also seemed to hold Jessie in high regard and had a fondness for her. Gil did not expect such gushing praise to come from a saboteur's messenger. Eventually Sam's sincerity and eagerness convinced him that the message wasn't a trick. The reference Sam made to Jessie's inviting him down to her Texas ranch added to his credibility. Gil didn't think there was a single man in the camp who knew Jessie had a ranch in Texas, and with a wry amusement Gil didn't think it likely that a saboteur would have such an obvious crush on her.

Gil had spent the remaining hours of the night riding hard, cursing himself most of the way for his original hesitation. As he reared up in front of his caboose, he told himself better late than never.

He knocked lightly at the door, not wanting to startle his sleeping sister. There was no answer, so he knocked again. An irrational fear started to grow in him, but he told himself she might have gotten up early and gone to help Pops prepare breakfast. But when he entered the car, he had his doubts about that. The bed looked unslept in and, even more upsetting, the chair was overturned.

He ran off in search of Jessie, but found no trace of her. He then raced to check the mess tent.

"Mornin', Gil, where's that young fella we sent after you?" Pops said upon seeing him.

Gil hardly heard him; his eyes were looking around frantically. "Where's Jessie? Where's my sister?" He fired off the questions quickly.

"Let's see now," Pops began, "the last I saw of Jessie, she was just finishing talking to all us. Don't know what she did after. I suppose your sister is asleep in the caboose."

"Well, she's not! Where's Spike?" He didn't wait for an answer, but ran off to find out for himself.

Spike's tent was empty. Gil didn't like the look of things. He began to stop the men who were walking by on their way to breakfast and asked them if they knew where Jessie, Spike, or Cynthia had gone. No one knew. Finally someone recalled overhearing Otto say he was "going to hit the breeze and had a special sendoff planned." Gil had a sinking feeling that his sister and Jessie were with Otto, and probably not of their own accord. He also had a hunch that they were on their way to Basin City; no other place would be suited for a proper "sendoff."

He went straight back to the mess tent and rushed up to a balding, potbellied man wearing striped overalls. "Peterson, I want a boxcar ready to be hauled in five minutes."

"It'll take twice that to build up steam," the engineer began to explain as he sat down to his plate of flapjacks. "And to couple a car from the siding'll take—" The engineer stopped as his plate of food flew across the tent.

"Just have it ready," Gil exploded. The men were looking at him curiously.

"Right," Peterson said a little uncertainly.

"It's important, Eddy," Gil added more calmly.

The engineer nodded. "It'll be ready," he promised and then rushed out.

In the meantime, Gil went to his caboose, dug out his Winchester, and dumped a box of shells into his vest pocket. He then went to the corral, brought out a fresh horse, and fixed his saddle to it. By the time he led the mount into the waiting boxcar, the engine was slowly backing its way down the siding. Gil smiled; he knew Peterson wouldn't disappoint him. He was just about to jump down and help couple the two cars when two workers approached him. He didn't recognize either of them, and although it was difficult to remember all the names, he knew that an unknown face was unusual. These faces were not only strange; they were unfriendly. Gil was already on his guard, even before they spoke their first hostile words.

"We don't think it's a good idea for you to be leaving, Gil," the first one said.

"Who are you?"

"The name's Jenks; this here's Burton." Unknown to Gil, they had both been in Spike's tent last night.

"Well, Mr. Jenks, why do you think it's not a good idea for me to be leavin'?" Gil asked sarcastically.

"There's been a lot of trouble with the men lately,

and for you to just hightail it, leavin' us here to do the work—"

"Well, it just ain't right," finished Burton.

Gil was eyeing them cautiously. He didn't think he could draw his gun and get the drop on both of them, but he had to make the first move while the element of surprise was still on his side.

"You boys are welcome to come along; I'm just runnin' in for some supplies."

"Well, that's mighty kind of you," Jenks began to say as he brought his hands up to stroke his whiskers.

This was the chance Gil was waiting for. If he acted quickly, he could strike before they could get to the guns he was sure were underneath their jackets. Taking hold of his rifle by the barrel, he swung it viciously at Burton's head and caught him squarely above the ear. Without waiting to see its effect, he launched himself at the surprised Jenks. They hit the ground together and started to roll. While Jenks was trying to reach into his pants to pull out his revolver, Gil kept pummeling his face with a strong right cross. But much of the power of his fist was diminished because both bodies were rolling in the same direction as the punch. They continued to roll, one on top of the other, as each of the men tried to get and hold the upper position.

Jenks had finally forgotten about his gun and was now trading punches with Gil. Although Jenks outweighed the locator, Gil had a slight advantage: His previous punches had bloodied Jenks' face and made a puffy slit of his right eye. Gil was sitting astride Jenks, assaulting his opponent's face with wild abandon, when a quick knee to his back threw him over. Gil was so intent on his attack that he was totally taken by surprise. Their positions were unexpectedly reversed, and a meaty fist struck him powerfully in the jaw. Suddenly there was a gun shot, and Jenks collapsed heavily against his body. The unexpected flip had saved his life.

Gil struggled under the dead weight of Jenks' body and pulled out his own revolver. Jenks' body offered him momentary protection from a second shot, but it also pinned him to the ground, helpless. Once out from under the body, he would have to aim quickly and accurately. He would only have one shot. With a powerful heave, he threw off Jenks and sat up.

He saw Burton stumbling forward, but didn't take time to question it. He fired two shots quickly and watched Burton drop. Only after Gil got to his feet did he see the whole picture. Peterson, shovel in hand, stood a few yards behind the dead Burton. Apparently, by the time Burton had recovered from his blow, the engineer had arrived on the scene. As Burton fired the shot that killed Jenks, Peterson hit him from behind. He was still reeling from the impact when Gil's bullets found their mark.

"Someone sure thinks it's important you don't get anywhere," Peterson noted as he poked at Burton's body with his shovel.

"Don't seem like what they think matters much, now does it?" Gil said as he dusted himself off. "You all set?"

The engineer nodded. "She's coupled and, by now, burstin' with the fever."

"Then let's get rolling," Gil said as he took hold and pulled himself up and into the small locomotive.

"Mind tellin' me what that was all about?" the engineer asked as he followed Gil into the engine.

"When we get up the steam, I'll explain it all."

To save on manpower, it was the general practice that whoever rode the pufferbilly would also act as the fireman. The pufferbilly, a much smaller locomotive used for short runs and light hauls, had an efficient boiler, and Gil soon had the engine up to full speed. And because of its light weight, when it wasn't pulling a load or, as in this case, pulling a very light one, it could rival the speeds of the more powerful workhorse engines.

Gil leaned on the shovel and wiped his sweaty brow with the back of his hand. "I think we're about to put a stop to all this sabotage."

"Those two men?" Peterson asked.

Gil nodded his head. "I think so. Why else would they try to stop me from leaving?"

Peterson thought it over briefly. "It's a good thing that it's about to end. I reckon the men have had about all they can take. Why, if it weren't for Jessie last night—"

"Why, what happened?" Gil cut him off quickly. "What did she do?"

Peterson retold the events: the attack on the workers, the strike Spike hoped to instigate, and the stirring speech Jessie delivered to the men. He capped it off by telling Gil, "She did a fine job of keepin' the men together. I doubt you could have done better." He started to blush. "But, of course, you wasn't there," he stammered self-consciously, hoping Gil would not take his remark as an insult.

"It's all right, Eddy," Gil said with a reassuring smile. "She can be a very persuasive woman. It's lucky for all of us she was there." He paused a moment. A dark thought crossed his mind. "But I'm not sure it was so lucky for her," he said somberly.

"What do you mean?"

"Well, I think Jessie and Cynthia must have found out something about the sabotage and were caught in the process."

"But I thought you said those two oafs back there were—"

"They're only part of the gang," Gil explained.

"Then who has Jessie and your sister?"

"I'm pretty sure it's Otto. And I have a hunch Spike is involved, too. I don't know if they're together, but they're both missing from camp."

"And right now we're on our way to head 'em off?" Peterson asked. Gil nodded. "How do you know which way they're headed?"

"Good question, Eddy. Which way would you head?"

"Basin City?" he said tentatively.

"That's my guess, too. There's also something else that leads me to believe that's where they're going."

"And that's . . . ?" Peterson prompted.

"I think the Oregon Central is behind the sabotage."

"With their office there, only a day's ride away, it's a good bet." Peterson's thoughtful tone changed to one of action. "Well, let's keep that fire stoked, boy," he said excitedly.

It required only an occasional shovelful to keep the boiler up to pressure. Gil had just placed the shovel aside when a question popped into his mind. "If Otto left last night, how far do you think he's gotten?" he asked his engineer.

"That's hard to say, Gil. What time last night?"

"Let's say midnight then."

"Midnight, huh?" The engineer did some quick calculations in his head. "Comin' up somewhere around Little Falls, I'd say. Of course, the earlier he left the farther along he'd be."

"And if he left closer to dawn, we'd have already passed him," Gil thought out loud.

"There's a stretch we're comin' up to that parallels the road for a piece. We could stop and you could look for tracks," Peterson suggested.

Gil gave him a sideways glance that had Peterson breaking into a chuckle. "Eddy, I wouldn't know the difference between last night's or last week's tracks. Would you?"

"I wouldn't know the difference 'tween last night's tracks and bear tracks," said the engineer. "I reckon we should leave the trackin' to the likes of Buffalo Bill."

"Or Ki," Gil said under his breath.

"And anyway, why slow her down when we got a full head of steam goin'?" continued Peterson.

"Right. I'd rather play it safe and head farther down the line than take the chance of missing them. We better go all the way to the Owl Creek trestle, even if I have to wait for them to show. Besides, the road's only about a quarter mile from the trestle."

"Okay," said the engineer. "But what's this *I* shenanigans. I'm in this, too."

Gil shook his head. "I want you to stay with the engine."

"But if Spike is with them, that'll make two against one. Not good odds, Gil," Peterson reasoned.

"I don't know that Spike is with them."

"But even so, why take the chance?" the engineer persisted.

"Eddy, you're the only member of the workers who knows about this. If anything were to happen to me, I wouldn't want those hombres to get away with it."

Peterson nodded. "I don't like the sound of it, but all right."

With nothing more to say on the subject, Gil scooped up another shovelful of coal.

The rest of the trip passed quietly, and before he knew it, Peterson was slowing down the train. "That's Owl Creek trestle coming up, Gil. Your mind still set on going it alone?" he asked.

"It is," Gil said firmly. "And if you don't hear from me in two days, send for the marshal."

"Good luck, Gil."

Gil climbed down from the locomotive. "Give me a minute to get my horse and then back it on out of here," he instructed.

Once in the saddle, Gil headed down to the creek. Following it south, he would soon link up with the road. He turned and waved to Peterson. The engineer gave a farewell toot on the whistle and threw the locomotive into reverse.

A short time later, Gil came to a flat, broad crossing in the creek. From here there was a road that snaked up the western embankment. It was not particularly steep, but the road, intended for wagon travel, switched back on itself many times before disappearing over the wooded hill. It was ironic, Gil thought, that the common sense used in carving this simple road was often overlooked by the builders of many defunct railroads. But this was not the time to indulge his pet peeve. He needed to find a position from which he could observe the road.

Just shy of the top of the hill, he saw a small outcropping

of rock, not more than thirty yards from the road. It would offer Gil both concealment and quick access down to any passing travelers. He made his way up to that spot and then tethered his horse to a shrub that lay hidden from the road. By climbing a little farther up the hillside, he had a good view of the road.

He was comfortably hunkered down beside a tree, wondering how long a wait he would have, when he suddenly saw the wagon come into view. The driver seemed to be the only occupant of the wagon, and he was too far away to make out his face, but the faded letters on the side of the baseboard were all too clear. There was no mistaking the W. R. R.—Wood River Railroad.

Jessie and Cynthia tried to get as comfortable as possible while they bounced and jostled in the back of the wagon. They soon discovered that if they relaxed and leaned against each other they could absorb most of the bumps without too much pain. They were tied tightly enough to restrict their movement, but not enough to cut off circulation. At the start of the trip, Jessie stayed wide awake, watching and waiting for any opportunity. But after a while she realized she wouldn't be able to repeat her earlier escape act; Spike rode in the back with them and remained cautious and alert. Finally, as dawn broke, Jessie decided a few hours sleep would do her more good than pointlessly staying awake. Later, she would need her wits about her, and she wouldn't want to have to demand quick reactions from a tired, sleepless body. As it turned out, she slept late into the afternoon.

She was startled awake by the sound of a distant steam whistle. Surprised as well, Otto turned around to Spike. "What was that? There isn't supposed to be a train comin' through here today." Spike didn't answer, and his silence further upset Otto. "You don't think something went wrong, do you?"

"I don't know," snapped Spike, "but we're not taking any chances." He spread open the canvas tarp that was folded in the corner of the wagon and covered the two women with it. "There's no need to tell you what'll happen if I see either of you pokin' your head out," he warned them. He then stretched out behind the seat, trying to be out of sight of any prying eyes.

Gil raced back down to his horse and got his Winchester. If he hurried, he would still have a clear shot. He scurried into position and, as he knelt against the boulder, brought the rifle butt up to his shoulder. The wagon was just rounding the bend and coming back into view. From this distance Gil could make out the features of the driver and had Otto dead in his sights. His finger began to squeeze the trigger slowly. He stopped abruptly. He lowered the rifle and went running back to his horse. He had almost made a critical mistake. First off, if Otto were alone, putting a slug through his head would kill any possibility Gil had of finding out where Jessie and Cynthia were. Second, Gil noticed that the back of the wagon was covered with a tarp. It was possible that the two women were tied up underneath it. If that were the case, shooting Otto would have an even more disastrous effect. Gil's shot would cause the horses to bolt and perhaps run off the winding road or topple over while going around one of the curves.

The only sensible thing to do was to force the wagon to a stop. If he could get down to the creek before Otto, he could lie in wait and then spring out just as the wagon would begin to make the crossing. He forced his horse down the embankment. He stayed off the road and took the shortest route, which was straight down. The animal half slid and half galloped down as it tried to stay ahead of the earth that crumbled beneath its hooves.

They made the bottom just as Gil heard the wagon start down the embankment. Because of the slope and the switchbacks, Gil would remain unseen until it was too late for Otto to do anything.

Gil drew his revolver and then waited a long impatient

moment before spurring his horse out. As he closed in on the wagon, he let off a shot into the air. "Rein 'em in," he shouted loudly.

As expected, the horses bolted at the sound of gunfire. Gil figured that while Otto was busy trying to get them back under control, he could easily get the drop on him. Much to his surprise, though, Otto gave the horses their head, and they dashed into the creek. Swearing under his breath, Gil kicked his horse into pursuit.

"Damn! It's Gil Johnson," Otto exclaimed.

"You just keep going," Spike barked from behind the seat. "I'll take care of him."

"We have not got much choice," Otto answered. "These animals have minds of their own."

As the wagon lurched forward, Jessie and Cynthia were immediately pitched back, but then they rolled forward and out from underneath their covering. Jessie had heard enough to understand the situation. She also had a clear view of Spike, who was kneeling on one knee and was slowly bringing his handgun up to his eye. It was obvious that Spike was waiting for Gil to get within point-blank range. She had no idea of how good a shot Spike was, but from his cool demeanor and his precise moves, Jessie had a feeling Spike didn't miss often. If Gil were pulling up alongside, or worse, trying to climb aboard, even the violent rocking back and forth of the wagon probably wouldn't save Gil from being shot.

Jessie threw herself face down into the wagon bottom, and at the same time twisted her back sharply. With herculean strength and a good measure of leverage, Jessie managed to flip Cynthia over her back. They had started their motion only a few feet from Spike, so Cynthia went crashing into the unsuspecting man, hitting him like a sack of potatoes. Jessie heard the gun go off. She hoped it was fired harmlessly into the air; Jessie was facing the wrong way to be certain. But when she saw Gil come diving into the wagon, there was no longer any doubt.

Now facing the rear of the wagon, she couldn't see what was going on, but she could hear what sounded like a humdinger of a fight. She felt a body fall on her; then she was suddenly grabbed by the hair and yanked to her feet. Spike, who had been at the losing end of a powerful fist and whose nose was bleeding badly, managed a detestable smile. Jessie found herself staring down the wrong end of his six-shooter. She let out a defeated sigh. Just as she had been forced to give in to Spike earlier, so, she realized, Gil would be forced to do now.

In the meantime, Gil was going to town on Otto. He was as fast with the punches as he was strong, yet Otto kept standing up to the punishment. It was only after an explosive right hook that Jessie realized that Otto was wedged in between the seat and the floorboard. There was no other way for him to keep to his feet. Gil was either unaware of this or unconcerned. He kept punching, stopping only to duck Otto's massive roundhouses. Jessie had not imagined Gil to be such a seasoned fighter and thought it a shame that it was all to no avail.

When it seemed a real possibility that Gil would beat Otto to death, Spike fired a shot into the air. Gil turned around quickly. It took him no time to figure things out; fear etched itself across his face.

The horses started to lunge forward again, but this time Otto brought them quickly to a stop. No one had fallen over; no one had even moved. Otto turned toward Gil, grabbed him by the shoulder, and took a powerful swing at him that caught him in the side of the jaw and lifted him clear off his feet. Dazed, Gil staggered to his feet, but flashed a quick smile at Jessie as if to show her he still had all his teeth. Otto went for Gil again; Spike stopped him. "That's enough Otto. There'll be time for that later."

Otto wiped the blood from the corner of his eye. Jessie thought Otto was going to disregard Spike's order. So did Spike. "We got business in Basin City," the foreman added.

"After tomorrow you can do what you want with him." Otto still looked undecided. "Besides, you want him to be able to see all the good things you're going to do to his sister here, don't you?"

Gil looked as if he were about to lunge at Spike when Spike cocked the hammer of his revolver and shook his head slowly. Gil leaned back on his heels. "You won't get away with this, Spike," Gil threatened.

"No?" Spike let out one of his ugly laughs.

"The train that brought me here has twenty armed men on it. They'll be waiting for you in Basin City."

Otto turned around quickly. "He's lying," Spike told him confidently.

"Am I?"

"Why would he tell us if it's true? He'd let us walk into the trap." But Spike sounded not all that certain.

"Because I want you to give up before they hang you for murder," Gil answered. "Quit before you go too far."

Otto had now stopped the horses. "Maybe we should forget Basin City, Spike," he said worriedly.

"He's bluffing, I tell you," Spike snapped back.

"Why would I be bluffing?" replied Gil. "Why would I come after you alone?" It was a question he wished he had an answer for.

Spike turned a shrewd eye to Gil. "How did you know about this?"

"Your friends Burton and Jenks," Gil answered confidently. "They told me you had my sister and Jessie and were probably heading this way to Basin City," Gil lied.

"Tie him up, Otto," Spike ordered. Both Otto and Gil looked confused. "No one knew we had these fillies. Least of all Burton and Jenks. That was my little secret. You just talked too much. Done saved our hides, too!"

Otto finished tying Gil and then gave him a swift kick in the ribs. Gil grunted in pain.

"Get those horses movin', Otto. I suddenly got a real

hankerin' for these two sweet things." Once again there was that disdainful laugh. Jessie tried to console herself by vowing that ultimately she would have the last laugh.

★

Chapter 16

Ki sat at a corner table of the Iron Rail saloon, picking at his steak dinner. The day had passed and little had been accomplished. Last night, after the incident in the railroad office, Stoney invited Ki to join him at Fannie's brothel. Ki politely passed up the offer and took a room at the hotel. The head thug would be nursing his wounds, and Ki was sure there would be no action to speak of from the others. For lack of anything better to do, he turned in early.

Ki rose at dawn, scouted out the railroad yard, and then spent the rest of the day watching the railroad office and the bank. He also asked many of the town merchants questions about both institutions. Unfortunately, he came up with nothing solid. He had many suspicions, but no facts to back them up. He had seen enough to suspect that the bank was financing the railroad, or perhaps the railroad was using the bank as a front. It didn't really matter; they were both crooked. The four thugs, supposed employees of the Oregon Central, were no doubt employed only as saboteurs.

But not only was there little solid proof, there were still

important unknowns such as who was giving the orders. Without knowing who the top man was, they would be battling a snake by cutting off its rattler. It could still strike, deadly as ever, but there would be no warning. They could kill the known cartel agents, but new ones would be hired to replace them. And it would be impossible to keep track of every new man. At least now they had a small advantage. They could keep an eye on the suspects and hope that eventually whoever was number one would show his face.

Time, however, was not on their side. If the sabotage continued unchecked, eventually the cartel would win. So far, Ki had managed to stop the cartel only after it struck and the damage was done. Ki was normally a patient man, but if nothing significant happened tonight, he was planning to head back to the Wood River railhead tomorrow morning. Things might be happening there that would need his attention. Besides, even if Jessie could take care of herself, Ki didn't like to leave her alone for too long.

Ki was just finishing his meal when the four thugs strode into the saloon. Ki smiled to himself. He would have preferred having a quiet dinner at the boarding house across the street, but it didn't seem like the type of place Baker and his friends would haunt. So he decided to kill two birds with one stone and eat in the saloon.

Baker noticed Ki right away and swaggered up to the table. "Well, if it isn't the Chinaman. I'm gonna wet my whistle. When I'm finished, you best be gone."

"I don't reckon he'll be so brave without that ol' coot by his side."

At the mention of Stoney, Baker reeled on his friend. "Remember, when you find that ol' buzzard, he's mine," he snapped as he rubbed his bandaged hand.

"We don't like to drink with your stink in the place," Curly added bravely.

"Savvy, mister?" Baker spat out the words.

"When I'm finished, maybe I'll leave," Ki explained calmly.

Baker slapped the plate of food across the room. "You're finished now!" he said and stalked off to the bar.

The bartender rushed over quickly. "You was practically done, mister. No sense causing trouble," he advised Ki as he picked up the broken plate.

"Gimme whiskey," Baker called loudly from the bar.

Ki turned to the bartender, but spoke in a voice loud enough for everyone to hear. "I'll buy his drink, but serve it to him in a bowl. I don't think he could hold a glass in his bandaged hand. Let him drink it like a dog."

Baker turned livid. "You just signed your own death certificate, mister," he bellowed across the room.

"He's a bad sort," the bartender whispered to Ki. "Why don't you hightail it outta here. By the time he finishes drinkin', the dust'll be settled."

"Ain't no place you can hide that I won't find you," Baker continued to rant.

"He means it," the bartender cautioned Ki.

Ki thanked him for his concern and then turned back to Baker, who was still shouting loudly. "This town'll be a better place when that scum's pushin' up dirt." Baker pointed his bandaged hand at Ki.

Somehow Ki thought the very same about Baker. He almost felt a touch of remorse about goading Baker into a fight, especially a fight that would prove to be his last. The frustration of the last few days was about to boil over. Ki was tired of being at the mercy of the cartel and their saboteurs. Jessie would not have approved, but then Jessie wasn't here. Ki now judged Baker to be expendable, as long as he had the other heavies to keep an eye on.

Ki had already slipped his hand into his vest and held two *shuriken* firmly in his grasp. He turned back to the bartender who was standing nervously alongside the table. "I'll have pie," he said flatly.

"What?" exclaimed the shocked bartender.

"A piece of apple pie, please," Ki said.

Ki was tense and ready when he saw Baker's eyes shift

briefly to the door. Out of the corner of his eye, he saw Spike McCaully push his way through. Spike was halfway into the saloon when he turned to follow Baker's stare.

"What are you doing here?" the foreman exclaimed.

"I could ask you the same thing," answered Ki.

"I thought you'd be long gone," Spike said with a smile.

Ki had a feeling he knew exactly what Spike meant and why he looked so surprised to see him. But he couldn't figure out why the foreman also seemed pleased to see him. Ki had no way of knowing that now Spike could rest easy, knowing that Ki was not, in fact, on his way back with a federal marshal as Jessie had warned.

"I had enough and quit," Spike said, explaining his presence.

"You're friends!" Baker bellowed from the bar.

Spike grinned maliciously. "Let's say we know each other," he said as he headed to the bar.

Ki was surprised to find out that Spike knew Baker, but as he thought about it, he realized that he shouldn't have been. It confirmed what he suspected all along. Spike and the four thugs went to sit at a far table. They were out of earshot, but Spike seemed to be doing most of the talking. Occasionally, Baker would nod his head and look at Ki. When they finished talking, Spike got up, grabbed a bottle of whiskey from behind the bar, and headed out the door. The others followed him.

Ki was not buying Spike's story about quitting. Something else had happened—something that involved violence; Spike's swollen and discolored nose attested to the fact. And it was something that also made Spike feel secure enough to flaunt his true allegiance in front of Ki. And anything that gave Spike the upper hand worried Ki. He had to find out what it was. He followed them quickly to the door.

Two men went with Spike and Baker; the other set out in the other direction. Ki got to the door in time to hear him call out to his friends, "Now be sure to save some for me, you hear? I'll be back tomorrow."

Spike nodded. "It'll be waiting."

Ki waited a moment and then stepped noiselessly into the night.

Ki raced after Spike a bit too eagerly. It was not very late, and Ki felt that if it were necessary he could duck behind one of the few people still walking down the street. It was when Spike and his gang turned down a side street that Ki made his mistake. It was natural for a person up to no good to look back over his shoulder periodically, and Ki should have realized that, as they turned the corner, there was a more than likely chance someone would take a cautious peek around. When Baker did just that, there was nowhere for Ki to hide.

"That son of a bitch is following us!" Baker practically shrieked.

"We'll take care of him once and for all," Curly snarled. "Let's go, Chuck."

Ki turned and ran. It would do no good to fight the whole bunch at once. To find out where they were heading and why, he would have to single one or two out and work them till he got the answers to his questions.

"Damned if he ain't turnin' yellow," Curly said with a chuckle. "But it won't do him a lick of good," he said as he took off in pursuit.

Ki raced down the alley that ran behind the stable, but was careful not to run too fast. He didn't want to lose the oaf. He sensed he had gotten far enough away from Spike and Baker, so he ducked behind a small pumphouse. A moment later he could hear the heavy footsteps and deep panting of his pursuers.

He stepped out from his hiding place. A quick strike brought his elbow deep into Curly's Adam's apple. He could hear the man gagging and coughing, but paid him no attention. He was already in the middle of a sweeping roundhouse kick that caught Chuck at the height of its extension and sent him reeling backward. Ki returned to Curly, who was still doing nothing more than trying to breathe. A kick caught him square in the face. Ki's second kick knocked Curly head first into the horse trough.

Chuck was in the process of drawing his gun when Ki came flying through the air at him. His legs clamped around Chuck's head and brought him down. Chuck was helpless and unable to move, but for added measure Ki released his leg hold just long enough to dig his heel into the thug's groin.

When his painful cries died down, Ki twisted their bodies around so Chuck could see his friend slumped, face down, in the trough. Curly had either been knocked unconscious before his face went splashing into the water or was knocked out as his head hit the side of the wooden trough. It was irrelevant, though, which way it had happened.

"Your friend won't be able to help. Do you understand?" Ki said slowly to his helpless captive. "You can wind up like him. Or you can answer my questions. Do you understand?" Chuck had no freedom of movement, but Ki could detect the slightest trace of a nod. He continued, "I want to know where you were going and why. You'll only get one chance to answer. Do you understand?" Again there was the faint, terrified nod.

Ki released his hold slightly. "To Fannie's." The voice was a weak rasp. "To plug a couple of petticoats Spike has hog-tied there."

"What room?" Ki demanded.

"I don't know. Maybe in the back."

There was nothing more to be gained. Ki placed his hand around the man's neck and dug his thumb and forefinger behind each side of his jaw. He squeezed firmly and carefully and Chuck slumped forward unconscious. Too heavy a touch on the very sensitive pressure points could result in a dead victim instead of a disabled one. Right now, though, Ki was hardly concerned with whether he had erred.

The wagon finally stopped. The cover was removed from

their heads, and Jessie, Cynthia, and Gil were led at gun-point into the back of a large house. It was dark out, and Jessie could see little before they were inside. They were ushered down a lushly carpeted hall into the first door on the right. Jessie didn't have to wonder where they were. The red carpet and decorative hanging paper were a dead giveaway. The room they were in was totally covered in heavy velvet drapes and had chains and leather harnesses bolted into the walls. Obviously they were in a bordello for the man of discriminating, if not sick, taste.

All three were summarily shackled to the wall. There were no tricks Jessie could employ here. Her legs were clamped, her wrists were held fast in leather cuffs, and a tight collar was fastened around her neck. There was even a bit ready to keep her silent. On the opposite wall, there was an assortment of whips and canes. Jessie shuddered. She could be grateful that she still had her clothes on. But she was not clinging to any delusions; she knew it was only a matter of time.

Spike, though, seemed preoccupied. Apparently there were things to be done first, and he seemed not to be in any hurry to indulge in his wicked pleasures just yet. It was obvious to all that this time they were going nowhere. Spike could get to them at his leisure. "Stand outside and guard the door," he instructed Otto. "I'll be back soon."

A moment later the three captives were alone and totally helpless. Jessie was unaware how much time had passed before Spike returned. Her mind was racing futilely for a way out, but so far had come up with nothing.

Spike and Otto stepped back into the room. From the hushed voices she heard, they had apparently left a third person outside to stand watch, Jessie surmised.

Spike pulled off his boots and then took a swig from the bottle he held. "You can do what you want to Cynthia, but she's mine," Spike said as he pointed to Jessie. "You might even like it, *Miss* Starbuck, if you like it rough, that is." He gave one of his hideous laughs and began to pull off his jeans. His manhood was already swollen and engorged. Jessie turned her head, looked away, and then caught her breath. She thought she saw something move behind the curtain. Was there an open window someone could have climbed in through?

Otto must have seen something, too, because he walked over to investigate. He was poking at the drapes with his six-shooter, looking for the opening between the drapes, when suddenly the fabric came toppling down on his head. Ki stepped out from the mass of fabric and gave a quick kick to Otto's head. Tangled in the fabric, Otto fell to the floor.

Ki then spun on his heels and swung his elbow. After a flick of Ki's wrist, the tiny silver throwing star spun across the room and embedded itself in the far wall. For a moment Jessie thought it had missed its mark. But then she saw the silver star was stained red. The *shuriken* had come to rest in the wall, but not before it had severed Spike's jugular. Spike stood there, dead on his feet, as blood dripped from the gash in his throat.

Meanwhile, Otto was trying to fight his way out from under the drape. Ki kept delivering explosive snap kicks to the struggling mass of red velvet. As Ki's foot again made contact, there was a muffled gunshot, and the body lay still. Otto must have had his revolver ready when Ki's kick caused the trigger to go off. The muffled sound would have been caused by the barrel pressing into Otto's body.

At the sound, the door opened, and Baker stuck his head in. "Everything okay?" he started to ask and then stopped abruptly as he saw Ki. He was holding a sawed-off shotgun and began leveling it at Ki. Ki's hands moved in a blur. Baker was holding the gun in his bandaged right hand and had his left hand on the trigger. He was quite capable of blasting, even with his hands reversed, but it was an awkward, unaccustomed move. The extra time it took to coordinate saved Ki's life. Before the gun was leveled, Baker fell over backward. One *shuriken* protruded from the center of his forehead; another pierced his eye. The gun never went off.

In the hotel parlor, Jessie, Ki, Cynthia, and Gil shared a bottle of fine brandy as they all retold their stories. They were relieved, but Gil still seemed ill at ease. "What's troubling you, Gil?" Jessie asked.

"Well, it seems we're not through yet. There are still other saboteurs loose. All we did was clean out some of the lair. Spike and Otto may be gone, but what about the others?"

"Don't worry, Gil," Jessie said with a smile. "It'll all be taken care of by tomorrow. See, the first telegram I sent was a coded message to Commodore Whiting. I asked him to send out his private car, unattended, except for a few Pinkerton detectives and a federal marshal. Then I sent another message to him telling him to come out at once."

Ki already had a smile on his face, but the others hadn't caught on yet. Jessie continued. "We're always at a disadvantage, being on the defensive. I felt it was time to turn the tables. I was sure that my telegram would fall into the wrong hands—"

"So you were setting up Commodore Whiting's private car as a decoy," Gil beamed proudly.

Jessie nodded her head. "The chance to kidnap the president of the railroad was too big a prize for the cartel to pass up."

"And from what Jessie and I heard, the trap's already sprung," added Cynthia.

"You know," mused Gil, "I'm rather sad it's all wrapped up. It'll mean you and Ki will be leaving us."

"Well, now, Gil, I reckon that at about the time you finish this railroad, the first snows'll already be falling. Some warm Texas sun might be a welcome change. Ki and I would be glad to see both of you anytime you can make it down," Jessie offered.

"That's mighty nice of you," Cynthia said with a warm smile to Ki.

"But getting back to business, about tomorrow?" Gil asked.

"All we have to do is round 'em up. But first a good night's sleep."

Cynthia moved closer to Ki. "Looks like I owe you again for saving me. Seems like you're making a habit of it," she whispered to him. "I just hope I can keep rewarding you for it," she said with a sensual smile.

Ki smiled back. "Jessie," Ki began, "maybe we can leave the roundup to the marshal and his men."

Jessie thought a moment and then smiled, too. "I don't see why not."

"Good. Then tomorrow I've got to return a burro and thank a friend for saving my life." He recalled Baker's awkwardness with the shotgun and had Stoney's well-placed bullet to thank for it.

"And I'll go retrieve my gun. It fell out when we jumped from the train." She let out a sigh. "By tomorrow night we'll be heading back to the Circle Star." She sidled up to Gil. "I'm not really tired," she whispered softly.

"Dinner?" Gil asked.

A sly grin crossed Jessie's face as she took hold of Gil's arm. Her green eyes twinkled seductively and her tawny blond mane shimmered as she shook her head no.

Watch for

LONE STAR AND THE MISSION WAR

forty-sixth novel in the exciting
LONE STAR
series from Jove

coming in June!